Terry Aulich

CLAPPERLAND

Black comedy or political thriller?
At the End of Days, you choose.

First Edition published by
Australian Centres of Excellence—Aulich & Co. 2020
Copyright © 2020 by Terry Aulich

ISBN 978-0-6488265-0-7

Cover and layout by *Mouse & Mind*.
www.mouseandmind.com.au

For Luise

Contents

ONE

Every good gift

I avoid meetings like the plague. No good can come of them. Look at Macbeth and Julius Caesar and the debacle that later became known as the Salamanca Incident.

But my competitors in the public relations world were crowding around us, buying up regional media and hiring smart kids who actually understood Facebook. Change was out there in the early summer air and I knew we had to adapt like Darwin's iguana so I could pay the rent on our central Hobart office and the three staffers that demanded recompense every fortnight. So, I had this meeting already booked but there was this little problem on the way to the office.

"He's got a gun and he does the drugs." Lenny Lucic said. He was standing outside his restaurant like a shag on a rock as the morning traffic took testy people off to unsettling jobs. He was in his morning outfit, big black tie and suit like burnt charcoal. He was my best client since he owned four restaurants and a swag of pubs with pokie licenses. He had a bad habit of creating issues, which was good news for us.

"Who's got a gun?" I said.

"That new chef I hired. He's got a gun."

"Lenny, if I cooked like him I'd carry a gun."

"Yeah, yeah, mate. He's been sleeping in the bloody restaurant. What are you gonna do about it?" He tucked the white handkerchief back in his top pocket. Lennie was a sweater, meaning when he was worried, his Mediterranean skin ran like the Miljacka River where he grew up.

I looked at my watch. I had an appointment. A possible new client.

"Lenny. You got a chef who carries a gun. You don't pay me enough to go in there." I said.

Lenny mopped his brow again. "And he breaks my plates. Every time I make the criticisms he breaks a plate, right there in front of me."

I looked through the windows of The Balkan and couldn't see the crazy chef but, if he had a gun, I was prepared to give Lenny a discount so I could make my appointment on time.

"I'll call you." I said and was about to grab my double parked car when Dinny Dinham arrived in his unmarked Hyundai. Dinny heaved himself out and began his slow authoritative walk towards us.

"Lenny, you called me, then you called the cops?" I said.

Lenny wiped his lips with the steaming handkerchief. "Mate, I called them just in case that mad bastard shot you."

I tapped him on the forehead, lightly. "Lenny, thanks for caring. I'm off."

"Yeah, you'd better piss off." Dinny Dinham said from fifty metres away.

"Morning Detective-Inspector. What good ears you have." I said.

Dinny was solid in every way. Tight suit and thick flower power tie and hair that had cornered the last bottle of Californian Poppy in the world. He was also a sort of best mate as they say in the trade.

"I'll handle this." Dinny said. Then he added, "Not a word, OK?"

"I've got an appointment" I said.

"Goodo!" He said and gave me a child-like bye, bye wave.

When I left and navigated Hobart's five minute traffic jam, Dinny was walking with his arms around Lenny's shoulder like a father figure bringing hot chocolate at bed time.

I was only ten minutes late but I avoided Donna's eyes. She was a good girl but she always made me feel guilty because she was a good girl, with standards.

"Pastor Rayfinger and Mrs. Rayfinger are in there. I offered them coffee like you said but they don't drink it." She said as if that was a brownie point in heaven.

My staffers, Helen Troy and Robert Malahide were chatting with the potential clients. As usual, Helen and Robert were not fazed by me being late.

"O.K." I said and sat immediately without shaking hands but I did the usual generous wave that said *don't get up*. It's called the God touch in some circles and bad manners in others but in the world I worked in, it was Advertising Rule Number One that I got from my old man who set up the firm and was full of vague aphorisms and vaguer rules. *Be late and your fees go up*. When we were all nice and comfortable and the half standing and half sitting was over I said. "Where do we start?"

I looked straight at Pastor Tommy Rayfinger and his diminutive wife, Tammy. The words *perfectly formed* came to mind. Clean, non-smoking skin, alcohol free lips and clothes that hovered between trendy and buttoned up. Tailored jeans, floral shirt and a dress topped with an embroidered collar and brooch. His and hers.

I had Donna's note in front of me which told me that the Rayfingers and the *Coming Now* Church ran a church youth club, a speed boat club called the Girl Power Boat Club and another club called the Electric Evangelicals which catered for model train enthusiasts.

3

Both the Rayfingers were in their late thirties and curious. They had already given our office a furtive once over. The Colonial Mutual Building was actually a surprise for most of our clients. Patrick Kennedy and Associates didn't go in for glass and steel modernity. We were comfortable in that six story Spanish mission building with its tiled roof, Art Deco glass doors and furniture to match. In twenty years we had replaced nothing, which said a lot about our company. *When you get it right, you get it right we used to say*, before the competition started knocking off our clients like May flies in the breeding season.

"Well we can cut to the chase and talk turkey." Pastor Tommy said in an eerie, rumbling voice that brought Charlton Heston back from the dead. He had the same granite face too but the jet black bouffant hair was all his. He leant his lanky figure so far forward he could have laid his hand on my shoulder. Then he paused, like a practiced public speaker and added as if he was translating the Dead Sea Scrolls for beginners. "We're talking here about politics and the Holy Bible." He leaned forward even further to let that wonderful thought sink in.

I knew Pastor Tommy could lean and reach because I was a football fan and Tommy Rayfinger was the greatest fullback in the Australian Football League until he suddenly left one day, went to Bible College in the US and emerged a full blown preacher with a congregation bigger than the St. Kilda Football Club.

"Yes, politics and the Holy Bible," I said and waited while Helen Troy and Robert Malahide opened their lap-tops. They were my alpha team and, lately also my beta and gamma and epsilon team. They could track and hack every computer, touch up any photos or videos and turn villains into saints so that Patrick Kennedy and Associates were once *the* go-to office for public relations in the state; that was before I took some wrong turnings of a personal nature.

Pastor Tommy waved his hands briskly at Robert and Helen. "No notes, no notes. It's kimono time."

I looked discreetly at Helen. Her background in the SAS and a few tours in Afghanistan and Iraq had fashioned a face that habitually betrayed nothing.

Men who talked about opening kimonos made me edgy but business was business and we were all dying to know why the hell the Tommy and Tammy team had sought us out. So I leaned back in my chair and began the show.

"So Pastor Tommy and...Mrs. Rayfinger..."

"Tammy." She purred and held Tommy's hands like a Prime Minister's wife, or at least those wives on the conservative side of politics. She had a soft accent from the American South.

"And Tammy," I corrected myself, "Politics and the Holy Bible? Are you sure it's Patrick Kennedy and Associates you want? You see, we aren't big on church things and some people say we're a little too close to the uh, progressive political parties." A better way to put it would have been, *the state and federal Liberals have blackballed us*, but no point in worrying Team Rayfinger with trivial detail.

Tommy Rayfinger clapped his hands. You couldn't help but be fascinated by their size, like a steamroller had passed over them. Then that Charlton Heston voice again. "That is exactly why *Coming Now* wants you on our team." He opened his big brown eyes and kept them on me, unblinking, watching my reaction." You see, that's the whole point. We want a team that isn't buddy buddies with the Liberal Party. Nope. We're the outsider's team. What we want to do, requires *you*." He pointed his long finger at me, hesitated, then pointed the same finger at a surprised Helen and Robert.

Tammy Rayfinger crossed her legs delicately and nodded in her husband's direction. The simple blue dress with its high collar strangely suited her, making her look younger or was it the fringe on her short, bobbed black hair? But then, a closer look told you she was wearing more make-up than Myer and the gold bracelets weren't preacher's wife material.

"Letting Australia know that we have, right here, a genuine real man for real people." She said and gave her husband another glance as if admiring the strong nose and carefully managed hair.

Tammy Rayfinger was an accomplished breather too. Way up there in the breathlessness stakes. Every word emerged with a steady stream of beautifully articulated air, and, the eyes made you feel that every word you uttered was just poetry. True Pastor's wife stuff.

Politics and the Holy Bible. There was a lot of it around those days. Telling everyone else what to do was back in fashion so why not Tommy Rayfinger? A political campaign revolving around this man? A Tommy Rayfinger public relations juggernaut. A real man for real people but it was also a man not like other men but like a God that had been bred in a different stable from ordinary mortals. It was a statue outside the MCG type of strong nosed hero for nine year olds, the type you recognise in a crowded airport. A leader amongst us. But what if he was as thick as a brick and couldn't afford our fees? Or just plain nuts.

"So just to put you in context. You're a bit like Hill Song?" I said, dipping our corporate toe into the River Jordan.

Tammy drew her head back sharply as if I'd thrown a gym soaked towel at her "No, no, no, Mr. Kennedy. We are definitely not Hill Song. Oh no, we are here for a very different purpose." She quickly glanced at her husband, encouraging him to set that straight.

"So what is it exactly that you want us to do? You know, the purpose?" I said.

Pastor Tommy smiled benignly. "The purpose? For the purpose of becoming the Liberal Member for Lyons in the Parliament of our country." He announced it like Moses, in capital letters, good TV preacher stuff, prowling the stage with those face microphones that looked like beauty spots. But an evangelical preacher in Hobart reaching the green leather seats of Parliament House Canberra probably required a few more tricks than burning bushes or parting the Red Sea.

"Uh, huh. So we make that possible?" I said and looked secretly at my watch. Helen and Robert shifted uncomfortably in their chairs. I noticed Tammy Rayfinger surveying Helen's T-Shirt and cargo pants. She was obviously more impressed with Robert's ability to wear a three piece suit in summer without sweating.

My battered mobile phone buzzed. There was a text from Lenny Lucic. "Call me urgent." I ignored it until Donna, the receptionist, poked her nose through the doorway and, almost bowing to the Rayfingers, dropped a note on my desk. "Call me urgent, Lenny".

"Excuse me. I'll need to take this call."

In Robert and Helen's office I tried to find a chair that didn't have files or a spaghetti farm of cables and speakers. Someone had locked the filming studio because we were hiring it out so I sat on Robert's desk.

"Lenny. I'm in a meeting." I said.

"And good day to also you my friend."

"Touché. What's the problem now?"

"Nothing. But that cop says he knows you and I gotta shut up about my chef with the guns and the drug."

Some of Lenny's restaurants were good enough to rate great reviews, although Patrick Kennedy and Associates had helped organise a few. We gave up on the pubs but, to be fair, we did give some decent advice about capitalizing on Tassie's wine and food renaissance. Which meant Lenny drove out every Sunday to the Coal Valley and tried to beat the wine makers down while he drank his own profits. So, it was time for more advice.

"Lenny. Mate. Take a vow of silence. That'll save your plates.

Otherwise, what can I do? You don't pay us enough to disarm crazy drug dealing chefs."

"No, no mate. But you got friends in you know where."

"I'll try and put in a good word. You want him moved on, like discreetly?"

"Yeah mate. I am in fear, right now."

"Fear! You survived the civil war in Sarejevo and you're in fear in Hobart! Jeez Louise! But, as for your gun loving chef. Consider it done. By the way, that Veal Marsala. The meat was clucking."

"Yeah, yeah, we ran out of veal. I'll make it up to you. Love you like a brother, mate."

In the reception area Donna was still monitoring the news on commercial TV. A political advert by Clive Palmer was followed by another ad where the announcer promised that *the Sleepmakerpro passes the raw egg under the mattress test*. It felt like a day that needed a miracle.

Tommy Rayfinger was explaining to Helen and Robert the reason why the Gospel of Prosperity worked with people who weren't rich but didn't want to lose what they had. I knew it was fascinating because Robert said uh, huh about three times and kept adjusting his cufflinks.

"So where were we?" I said.

"That's only the first part. There is more." Pastor Tommy said as if there's been no Lenny Lucic or no detour into the Gospel of Prosperity.

Helen and Robert looked relieved although Helen disguised it better.

"What is more?" I asked.

"I need to be Prime Minister." He sat back and waited for my reaction, as if birds were about to fall from the trees.

"And I want to paint like Da Vinci, Pastor Tommy. We've already got a PM who can clap hands and call on God to favour Australia. How about Secretary-General of the UN?" I said. *What the hell?*

Tommy Rayfinger gave me that eerie other planet gaze. "No, the Word of God begins in this country, right here in the Apple Isle, right here in this orchard." he said.

We had lawyers climbing all over us and clients were disappearing faster than Usain Bolt. That day, Patrick Kennedy and Associates were looking for good solid clients who paid big and long and probably wouldn't recognise an angel if they tripped over one.

We needed a gift and, instead we had a circus called the Rayfingers.

I got up and went to the window. Down on the Harbour, the MONA Roma ferry, camouflaged like an attack craft, manoeuvred into position ready to load visitors to MONA, the wayward museum that was pulling in visitors like hundreds and thousands on bread at a kids' party. Even Americans off the great cruise ships who'd paid for five meals a day up front got on the ferry. *Twenty five bucks for Chrissakes when you could get a bus out there for four dollars and how come they don't charge the locals an entrance fee and don't they have this blasphemous festival in midwinter where they hang crosses upside down and didn't they bury a guy in a breathing box under the street with the traffic running over him, what kind of town is this?*

It was a fine early summer day and the green leaves of the oaks in Franklin Square were tickling the sky. I sat down again and moved the Onyx naked woman holding the Art Deco lampshade so that I could get a better view of Tammy Rayfinger. *Holiday camps, bonfires on the beach and terry toweling shorts, alpha girl in her day.*

I tried again. "Well, are you sure we're a good fit? You've already got a good message but resources, well..."

Pastor Tommy chuckled from deep in his throat. He adjusted his black tailored jacket with surprisingly delicate movements.

"Message! Our message has been tested over the last two thousand years." He let that momentous statement sink in. "As for resources, we have resources a plenty. Don't doubt that."

I was still hovering between doubt and belief and I came down on the side of doubt. I shook my head.

"Look, Pastor Tommy and Mrs. Rayfinger, it's been an interesting offer. Frankly, we don't do religion round here and I don't see a compelling reason to change that." That seemed to make both Robert and Helen happy. I could tell that because they sat like Buddha, suppressing all emotion, especially relief and joy.

Pastor Tommy just smiled at me that then shuffled his big hands inside his jacket and fished out a cheque book followed by an expensive looking fountain pen. He opened the cheque book, wrote on it carefully and handed it over with a theatrical flourish.

"Would that be a compelling reason?" He said, still smiling.

I looked at the cheque. *Pay Patrick Kennedy and Associates the sum of two hundred and fifty thousand dollars* it said in neat clear writing. The cheque had a line under the CAN which said *Coming Now Incorporated*.

I put it down. "OK. That's a pretty good reason. Can you give me another reason?"

Pastor Tommy shrugged and went through the routine again. This time the figure was two hundred thousand. I looked at Helen. Her snub nose was disdainful but fascinated in a ghoulish way. Robert crossed his legs and stretched his neck, a sure sign he was perplexed.

I took the cheque and added it to the other. A man who uses a cheque book had to be of a serious purpose as they say in the classics.

"I really need another good reason." I said. Inoffensive. Gentle.

Pastor Tommy sighed and came up with another fifty grand. "I think that's reason enough." He said firmly. Tammy Rayfinger stiffened and raised her finely applied eyebrows.

I did not look at Helen and Robert. I already knew what they were thinking but they weren't paying the rent.

Pastor Tommy and Tammy were watching, waiting. On that day, I had no idea what money circulated in churches and how much got sent to God and how much stayed at home, if you get what I mean. I usually checked out my clients before I meet them; trustworthiness, their background and of course, their capacity to pay. But with the *Coming Now* church I hadn't taken them seriously before that meeting.

"OK", I said, "We'll think about it seriously."

Tammy Rayfinger crossed her legs and gave me that marshmallow pie smile. "How *seriously* Mr. Kennedy?"

I thought about the cheques burning a hole in my desk, the desk that I'd wrestled from the hands of an avaricious Paris antique dealer in the days when we had offices in Sydney and Melbourne and Friday lunches began on Thursdays.

"Very seriously. But I'd need to have a look around your organization first and create a strategic plan that might sharpen the focus on those big goals of yours" I said. I liked that part where we spoke fluent business speak with those clients who paid up front. That was Advertising Rule Number Two, *Make Simple Things Look Complex and Charge Accordingly and Often.*

Tommy Rayfinger stood up. The act of standing up seemed to take a long time and his broad shoulders seemed to get broader. Pastor Tommy was still in fighting fit condition, lean and commanding, the kind of physique that evoked respect from those who didn't eat their vegetables as kids and wouldn't know abstinence if they tripped over it.

"OK. How about the Compound this time tomorrow?" He rumbled.

Tammy touched him lightly on the arm. "Don't worry about him.

He always calls our little Church and its admin block the Compound. Here's our card but I expect you already know where to find us."

"Absolutely," I lied.

Pastor Tommy shook my hand as if it was a floppy doll and he needed to do all the work. Tammy offered hers with a gesture straight out of the etiquette books. They nodded at Helen and Robert. Helen didn't get up but Robert the Polite came close to kissing Tammy's hand.

Tammy ran her fingers quickly over my desk and took a sideways glance at my naked lady lamp. "Just love your taste in furniture Mr. Kennedy. Just love it. We like someone who's enjoying the fruits of his labour, don't we honey?"

Tommy nodded his head as if he was thinking that one over. His eyes avoided the lamp. "Oh yes. Those that have a go, get a go. Oh, yes sir!" Then he recovered himself and gave us a thumbs up as they headed for the door. In the doorway he stooped slightly as if the room had shrunk while we talked. "I am predicting that we will have a long and fruitful relationship. I can see it plain as day." He stood back gallantly to allow his wife to pass through the doorway. She acknowledged his good manners with a slight nod as if they were already entering the green marbled halls of Parliament.

Soon there were just three of us and a lingering scent of expensive perfume.

Helen leant back in her chair and exhaled like a diver coming up for air. "Phew!"

"Don't lean back on my Biedermeir." I said.

"Bieder smeeder!" She said and crossed her arms over her head. "The Tammy and Tommy show. Have you ever seen anything like it?"

Robert opened his laptop and keyed in a search. He was chortling or whatever describes a comedy session shared only with oneself. "Oh, dear. You should have warned us. Did anyone actually Google them before we made the appointment?"

He looked around with a mild accusatory air. "I thought not. I must say I enjoyed the hand-holding. Rather sweet, don't you think? So, may I get back to my desk?" *A camera is a traitor to truth* said a sign above Robert's desk. I never figured that one out, since I never heard an animal tell a lie and Robert spent most of his career as a wild life photographer in Africa before he drifted to Hobart in a cloud of mystery.

Helen was about to get up but I gestured for them to sit again. I tapped the desk and held up the three cheques. "Well you better get used to Tammy and Tommy. I'm telling you now, if these little babies don't bounce we will be working for *Coming Now* Incorporated or Proprietary Limited or partners or whatever it's called."

Robert gave one of his Sergeant Wilson twitches, the British upper class sign when faced with troubling news. It's a slow twisting of the neck and eye rolling, as if you've slept badly. "Look, if you don't mind, I'd like to opt out of this one."

Helen slammed her laptop shut. "Not so fast, Tonto. I'm due for a vacation soon and I'm not..."

"You don't have any leave left." I said. "Now, on this one, it's the Three Musketeers or nothing."

Helen was suddenly on her feet. When agitated, she could move like a panther. She'd spent years in command driven organizations where life and death were daily twins but she had an Old Queensland frontier independence. That was before freckled face kids like her left as the little towns got smaller in every way.

"I wouldn't work for those bible bashing hypocrites if my arse was on fire." She said.

"Tell me what you really think." I said.

"Well old boy, I'm with Helen on this one," Robert said cautiously. He tossed the cowlick on his well coiffured head. "Not that I would put it as crudely."

"Yes or no?" I said.

They both spoke together, "No!". Then Robert added firmly, meaning his cut glass accent got stronger "I am not comfortable with people who believe they are God."

"OK. I've heard you loud and clear." I switched on the intercom.

"Yes Mr. Kennedy?" Donna said. She was the only one in the office who did not call me Paddy, although it didn't exactly trip off Robert's tongue. Donna was what they used to call a sweet kid in the days when young women had glory boxes, a deposit on a house and a steady boyfriend that knew the limits before marriage.

"Donna, after lunch can you bring the last reconciliation statements and the Investment Fund books."

"Yes Mr. Kennedy."

"Oh, and Donna, bring the employee contracts with you." I said, picking up the cheques, making sure my sweaty fingers didn't blur the signature and payee amount. Who knew what miracle disappearing ink the Rayfingers and *Coming Now* might have used?

Hobart had never looked sweeter that day. It was the type of day when the *Mercury* would run the first of the summer photographs of happy kids trying not to shiver and the coming election campaign was still a phony war. Protesters were gathering in Franklin Square preparing to march on the elegant little sandstone Parliament House down the road and, although they carried placards pronouncing *climate mayhem* and *save the world*, you had the feeling that they would have written *please* if they'd had enough space. Most were young people with a smattering of veterans who did look a bit grimmer but in a comfortable way. The local coffee shop was still writing cracking bad puns on its white board. This one said *be happy, our coffee sucks* with a picture of those take-away cups with mouthpieces on them.

I handed the cheque over the bank counter and the assistant said, "How's Donna?" and pretended not to notice the amount. I took the receipt and re-read the numbers just to be sure.

TWO

Pieces of silver

In the afternoon, Donna brought the accounts. In the background the 24 hour news cycle ran the gamut of fires, flood and famine with a touch of election fever and other natural disasters like Donald trump. Donna did the listening for all of us. Saved time and emotional energy.

"Anything we need to know?" I asked.

"Oh Mr. Kennedy. There's been a ferry capsized in Mosul; that's in Iraq, and a lot of families have drowned."

"Donna, you don't have to follow *all* the news."

She looked hurt, "But, Mr. Kennedy, you specifically asked me to monitor all the news."

"All the relevant news." I said.

Almost stubbornly she said, "Two hundred innocent people drowning in Iraq, after all they've have been through with those horrible ISIS people. That is relevant."

"And what can you do about it?" The moment I opened my big mouth I knew I should not have said it. Donna stiffened then, being Donna, gave me the benefit of the doubt.

"Well, I *can* do something about it. I sent off some money to the Red Cross." She said.

"Put me down for a thousand." I said.

"Oh Mr. Kennedy. That's so generous of you! But..."

"We're all in it together, Donna, all in it together. Now, where the hell is Helen?'

Robert said, "Mellifluous" and I said, "What?" and he said "Where the hell is Helen? It's mellifluous."

"Mrs. Troy is at the gym. She's on her way." Donna said, which explained nicely her role at Patrick Kennedy and Associates.

We waited five minutes while Robert played with his iPhone looking for *Coming Now* and reporting the results like "They have 60,000 members and they love to fight the Devil and they run coffee shops and they have a club called the Girl Power Boat Club. Get it? Girl power boat. Speed boats."

"Got it." I said.

Helen finally arrived in her black Leotards and battered running shoes that always looked like she'd stolen them from the SAS when she resigned. Her long red hair was wet and stuck to her neck and freckled shoulders.

"Sorry, I thought you were late because you were changing." I said but I was glad she hadn't changed. "OK." I said. "I am a brilliant sleuth. Just brilliant. So I detected a certain reluctance about all of us working with enthusiasm for the Rayfingers and *Coming Now*. So, just to keep Team Kennedy motivated, let's open the kimono."

"Oh dear. That kimono." said Robert, sniffing. Elegant but it *was* a sniff.

"OK Donna, tell us about the accounts."

Donna stood there with her hair tied in a neat head-band and a 1950s dress that could have been retro or a resewn carry-over from her mother who still lived in the Huon Valley. Donna and her fiancée as she called him had already bought their block of land and were saving for the deposit on a place nearby. I sometimes congratulated myself for my little contribution towards the decent folk like Donna and Ewan who saved and scrimped and still donated to Iraqi orphans.

"Everything, Mr. Kennedy?" Donna looked shocked, like a Swiss banker being asked to hand your money back.

"Well you can tell us a little about the profit and loss accounts then maybe the annual reconciliation." I motioned to her to take a seat but she clung to the account papers like grim death. "Donna, are we broke or not?"

Donna look horrified. "Mr. Kennedy. You asked me not to discuss the accounts with…uh…anyone else."

"Well Donna, I am now asking you to let my colleagues know where we sit."

"Well, Mr. Kennedy, we made a loss last year of one hundred and fifty thousand, dollars that is."

Everyone in the room knew that figure would have been correct. Donna was only twenty one but a few years at TAFE and she was ready to run the State budget. No expense or deduction escaped her attention.

Robert opened his laptop, tapped in an entry and turned its screen towards me. There was a photo of my Beidermeir chair with a price tag of thirty thousand. "You can sell the Biedermeir." He said then laughed and giggled at his finest.

"How did we survive?" Helen said. It was a question that carried genuine concern for reasons that I won't go into.

"The Investment Fund. That's how we survived" I said. "It had investments returning…uh."

Donna didn't even look at the accounts. "Six percent."

"Yep. Six percent."

Helen looked squarely at me. "Where did it all go? I mean the losses."

Donna cast a wary eye at me. I nodded, "Well, the biggest item was the lawyers for the libel case against us, against Patrick Kennedy and Associates. Then there was the cancellation of TPGH contract which went to those competitors, you know the ones that want to buy out all the country newspapers and…"

"That's enough, Donna. They've got the picture." I had personally lost the TPGH contract through an unfortunate biblical liaison and Hobart is a small place.

"I'm in." Helen said firmly.

"In what?" I asked.

She laughed and went across and shook the cheques like they were betting tickets. "I'll work for that syrupy bastard and his Grand Ol Opry missus provided…"

"Provided what?" I asked.

She laughed, "Provided the cheques don't bounce."

Donna was stunned. I could tell this because her bottom lip almost trembled. No-one ever did the banking but Donna. "Mr. Kennedy. You banked cheques?"

"Yes. I used a map and found my way to the bank. Here is the receipt."

Donna took it gingerly as if it was about to explode. Then she looked at the amount. "Five hundred thousand. Are you serious, Mr. Kennedy?"

"Deadly serious."

"And this is them, the Rayfingers and *Coming Now*?" Donna's eyes were wide open. She shook her head as if the streets outside were Bethlehem and the Rayfingers the Magi.

"*Coming Now*. Still think it's a great marketing name." Helen said. "Do you reckon that Tammy and Tommy? She's so tiny and he's like a Greek God but one of the dopey ones. You know, the one that killed Hector," She left the question floating in the air.

"Achilles, he was a demi-God but stupid and a trifle up himself, killed Hector and dragged his body gratuitously around Troy, angered the other Gods." Robert's cut glass accent suited Homer but not the Tammy and Tommy show which had just given us five hundred thousand to make them famous. Still he had a grin on his face like a man who had been saved from leprosy. He swept his hair from across his brow. In the light it looked a little on the dyed side.

"You two. You're wearing out my furniture."

"Well. So I dig up everything about *Coming Now?*" Robert paused for a moment. "God knows what we'll find."

He packed his laptop and left the room. Through the open door I could see him tapping away, humming some opera that no music lover could ever recognise.

Donna followed, holding the receipt like the formula for making gold, which in a way it was.

I said to nobody in particular, "There was once an advertising PR real estate doob who became President. So these days, I think to myself, any well-organised idiot can become King. In the Land of the Blind et cetera, etcetera."

Helen was still sitting there.

"And?" I said.

She stood up and leant with both hands on my desk. I'd seen this agitation before.

"You didn't tell me about the financial situation." She said quietly.

"Just book entries. Nothing serious but I'll admit that maybe it would have been a bit ticklish if our guardian angels from *Coming Now* hadn't turned up. A type of miracle really." I said casually and tried to ramble. "Every good gift is from above or even thirty pieces of silver."

"That's not the point." She interrupted. Such green eyes.

"What is the point?"

"You bloody know."

"For Christ's sake Helen. There's something else isn't there? What *is* bugging you?"

She drew a breath and pulled out one of those mini-recorders that spooks attach to phones. She fiddled with it, trying to find the passage.

"Apart from you not telling me about our financials. It's him again. That's what's bugging me." She passed the machine to me and stood watching my reactions.

I switched the machine to play. It was the same male voice, probably drugged or drunk but the message was clear enough.

"Flick. Yep, it's me again. Your old friend from you know where. Just another friendly call. It's payback time for rats. Yep, but it won't be tonight or tomorrow. It won't even be you first up, Flick. It'll be a friend, then another friend until you run out of friends. Then it'll be the rat, which is you. Don't try to trace us because we're smarter than you. Always was, you fucking rat."

"You are not sleeping at home tonight," I said.

THREE

Until the day break

Helen Troy's parents must have had a sense of humour when they named her after the woman who started a ten year war.

It was a joke I made the first time we met. "I didn't start that war but I reckon I could have finished it," she said and she wasn't joking.

The night we first met I was playing our regular gig with a group of old has-beens at the Shipwrights Arms in inner city, gentrified Battery point. A quartet that knocked out a combo of rockabilly and punk poetry to more mature types that still hoped for a better world. For me it was way of apologizing for the things we did during the week. I swear it was not my choice to call the group *Ship Creek*.

That night the Shippies was crowded with regulars not the newly arrived gentry so we gave it all we had. I finished with one that Greg, the drummer and I wrote together which is why I remembered all the words.

> *"The rich man in his fortress*
> *The poor man at his gate*
> *Train us all like horses*
> *To just accept our fate*
> *Sorry, sorry, sorry, yuh*
> *You can kiss my old cigar."*

The crowd always joins in the chorus, a protester's cottage pie of Vietnam, the saving of the Franklin and Climate Change. Still, speaking of pies, the inevitable call for the Tassie Pie song rang out. It was a standing joke that we finished all gigs with that bloody song.

"Tassie Pie song!"

We waited for a while. I took a swig of something that tasted like beer, grabbed the microphone again and belted it out. We were a crap band that never made it but they'll still be singing that Tassie Pie song long after we're gone.

I had just started when I noticed a tallish woman, arms folded, leaning against the wall. She was wearing an outfit that looked a lot like an army uniform with rolled up sleeves and epaulettes. When she moved, the light from the lead light window played on her generously red hair. I almost forgot the words to the song.

"Tassie Pies, they hit the spot
In times of trouble they never lie
Hit the spot, got the lot
Good old Tassie Pie
Good old, good old Tassie Pie.

Wander the whole world over
From sunny France and Spain
To the cliffs of rainy Dover
You'll be coming home again
To get your Tassie Pie
Good old Tassie, Tassie Pie
Good old, good old Tassie Pie"

I finished and, while the band packed up, I met her half way across the room. I'm not sure who did the walking towards but there we were, just looking at each other as if there were no other people in that crowded pub. Clichés and crowded room came to mind but she spoiled the effect.

"You're no Frank Sinatra." She pursed her mouth and questioned me with the greenest eyes this side of Dublin.

"No. But Old Blue Eyes never had to sing the Tassie Pie song at every gig." I said and tried to think of a good line but I needn't have bothered. She looked straight at me.

"Paddy, I want to ask a favour." She shifted on one foot.

"Ask away," I said. Steady Paddy, I thought but it was too late.

"I want to fuck you and I want a job."

I thought about it for a split second. "In what order?"

She smiled, almost with relief, I thought. "You choose."

"My place or yours."

"My place, I reckon you're the untidy type."

Her place was in Taroona which is few miles from the Shipwrights Arms and has many of its houses nesting amongst the gums and she-oaks; solid scientist, doctor, artist, musician, teacher country where houses are a mix of early timber and late timber and a touch of Art Deco and don't get sold much and even the beaches are discreetly hidden amongst the rocks. It's river front territory without the Sydney prices and the fights between rich neighbours over harbour views.

The winding road followed the river at its widest point and moonlight was playing on the water and the soft bare hills on the Eastern Shore. I had time to take it in as she drove in silence which was strangely tense but calm, if you know what I mean.

The house was in bushland overlooking the cliffs and more bush loomed above it. The oil stained weatherboards had seen better days but the garden had magnolias, lemon trees and she-oaks as if the original owners had intentionally planned a secret garden.

"Humble home," she said. I agreed.

She locked the doors of the little four wheel drive, took a good look around then keyed in a security code. It seemed a strange ritual for law-abiding Taroona.

Inside was a total surprise, a minimalist IKEA showcase with middle-eastern rugs scattered everywhere.

"You just ordered all of this? Looks brand new"

She smiled, "I do neat."

"So do I." I lied.

She poured two glasses of water and handed one to me.

"No you don't do neat, I can tell." she said firmly then, to dispel any doubts, she nodded towards a door. "Bedroom's in there."

She followed me in. There was a futon and doona on the floor, a simple cupboard painted a dull yellow and one poster advertising Casablanca. Nothing else but Bogey and me and Bogey was no competition any more.

Helen Troy was definitely a minimalist which she proved by removing her jacket, black T-shirt and Blundstone boots until she was naked, sitting on the bed. She patted the futon.

"I'm not used to this." I blurted out. Christ Paddy, I thought, this isn't the confessional.

"Your first time?" She laughed, her teeth glistening.

"First time I've actually been invited." I lied but, in strange way, it was not a lie.

She laughed. "You are a liar."

I dropped the rest of my clothes and lay down beside her while we touched each other's bodies without haste. Her long red flaming hair fell haphazardly across her shoulders and breasts.

"You are so..." I started.

She touched my lips gently and shook her head slowly. "No talk. You can talk by touching me."

We touched and murmured, simple natural movements without self-consciousness and soon I was moving inside her and feeling the almost isolating moments of two people who have only just met but were already intimate.

To this day, I don't know why that bare room, the futon on the floor and the trees outside catching the moonlight was as different as anything I had felt in my life.

Later, we lay on our backs and I could hear the light river breeze riffle the leaves outside. Out there thousands were sleeping while we floated together like sailors at sea.

Suddenly she said in a sleepy voice. "You can go now...if you want."

"I don't want."

"OK. But you've got to go before morning."

"The neighbours won't mind. They're artists and doctors."

She laughed and playfully slapped me on the arm. "I thought so. You are an idiot."

I got up to get a glass of water. There was enough moon-light in the lounge room and kitchen to take a good look at the lay-out. There was a single photo on the mantel-piece of what looked like an ancient fort probably in Afghanistan or maybe Northern Pakistan. It had been fortified with modern concrete barriers and rolled barbed wire.

"Don't touch that." She said quietly but urgently and retrieved the frame from my hands.

"You were in the army?" I said.

She frowned. "Yes, Mr. Stickybeak. SAS, signals officer. I wrote code and set out the attack co-ordinates for air strikes and drones."

"And now?"

She smiled bleakly. "And now I've gone walkabout, resigned, become human again." She folded her arms over her breasts.

"Still want a job?" I asked, I don't know why but I've always been the type who collects; people, objects, you name it, I collect like a swallow in spring.

"You are serious?" she said a little incredulously.

"Best job application I have ever had," I immediately regretted saying that as the smile line turned into an anxious frown. "Um, no security, crap salary but...a lot of appreciation. You start tomorrow."

It was destined.

"OK, tomorrow. But we keep tonight our little secret."

I touched her on the cheeks. "Helen Troy, I reckon, you keep a lot of little secrets."

She seemed taken aback but then took my face in both hands staring intently with those lapus lazuli green eyes. "I could say the same about you Paddy Kennedy, Tassie Pie man. Bloody Tassie Pie man! That is the worst song in the world. The worst." She was still laughing from time to time, even hours later.

FOUR

Building the temple

Helen and Robert worked all morning on the *Coming Now* project. They searched for *Coming Now*'s congregation numbers and compiled lists of publicly known members from Facebook and other social media posts. My door was open because of the steamy weather and I could hear them complaining about the job and bickering about who should do the bulk of the work.

Helen didn't like politics or religion and Robert was a sphinx about his private life. But we were on a tight schedule and, as incredible as Tommy Rayfinger's ambitions were, there was five hundred grand in the bank to make them credible.

"He's just a dumb arse. Look at this," Helen was saying. They were leaning over her laptop, sharing some of the wisdom of Pastor Tommy. She read aloud. *"Homosexuals are not evil people, just a little bit out of whack with God's plan."*

"Hmm." said Robert as if she'd been reading from Tommy's *Cook Book for Students Helping Mum.*

"Do you get pissed off when you read that sort of stuff?" Helen asked.

There was a pause. "Why do you think that is relevant?" Robert said.

"Well, you know, you are over forty, you're a pretty good looker in an upper class Pommie kind of way and you're not a short arse but you've never talked about women. And we're now working for a bunch of religious gay haters."

"I'm not gay, if that's what you mean."

Helen laughed. "Not just a little bit gay?"

Robert pondered. I knew that silence well. It said nobody owns me. Then I could see him assessing Helen, his finely chiseled features and sun tan were framed in the window light. There was a faint sign of a smile.

"Well, if I were to be a little bit gay, you can blame it on the fact that I was sent to a boarding school when I was seven and my mother burnt my rocking horse. That's why I spent a lot of my life in Africa photographing real life animals. And she also had my room repainted, in bright yellow as it so happens."

Helen said, "Seriously?"

Robert shrugged amiably then laughed at Helen's bewilderment. "Who knows about these things? Who knows the crimes we commit in our heart?"

Tammy Rayfinger had described their headquarters as a *little church and admin block*. Judging by the size of its headquarters in aptly named Bagdad, twenty minutes from Hobart, *Coming Now Incorporated* must have grown overnight like a Chinese housing development.

A line of flags topped by the Australian flag fluttered in the afternoon breeze. A large building stuccoed in earth colours featured two large white columns at its entrance. Behind were four large airport hangers from which a succession of staccato high pitched buzzing swelled and died erratically.

On the far right was a church structure with a giant dome half made of stained glass. Its Arabic features were modified by a giant cross and a sign which pronounced THE LORD SHALL PRESERVE THY GOING OUT AND THY COMING IN.

Below it, to assist the slow witted, was a smaller sign that announced COMING NOW: YOUR FAITH AT WORK.

It fitted perfectly a region where the early settlers tried to bless their theft of aboriginal land by calling their towns Bagdad, Jerusalem, Jericho and the Jordan River. In an area where Evangelicals built little sandstone chapels and others made money and built big sandstone mansions by kissing the Governor's backside, *Coming Now* fitted the tradition like a pile of prayer books.

Robert had done his homework and we were well briefed about *Coming Now* but we were still in for some surprises.

Helen whistled. "Well, looky, looky. Two years ago there was nothing here but empty paddocks. These boys and girls have been really working."

"Working like unpaid elves." Robert said grimly.

The car park was full and the lawns were manicured and cleanly edged. Well-watered hydrangeas, camellias and silver birches were artfully arranged around a number of boulders and some park benches.

To the far left, playing fields, tennis and basketball courts led to what we knew to be school buildings. A large sign said COMING NOW CHRISTIAN SCHOOL.

"Our taxes at work." Helen said.

"Careful, your politics of envy is showing like a pink slip." Robert said.

She didn't look at him. "Oh Defender of the Faith are we now, Lord Robert?"

"Stop it you two, here's the welcoming party."

Pastor Rayfinger was standing like his mate Moses on the steps of the large administration building. Beside him was Tammy, the picture of hospitality. Her floral dress fitted the nice mum picture and she capped it off as usual with an occasional admiring glance at her much taller husband.

Pastor Tommy stepped forward in his tight tailored jeans and Hawaiian shirt. We exchanged happy families and admired the gardens and tried to make ourselves heard above the noise of the half dozen medium sized drones that had mysteriously appeared and were hovering over us. Helen kept casting a wary eye on them. Pastor Tommy noticed her apprehension.

"Don't worry about them. Some of our geeky boys and girls are doing wonderful experimental work. Good work, good young people." he said as if that explained the presence of those hovering eagles.

"Big payload?" Helen asked.

Pastor Tommy smile indulgently at her. "The bigger the better. We've got big plans for these little wonders. Big plans. Please. Come into our humble abode."

I stood aside to let Tammy Rayfinger through the door when a high pitched spluttering sound came on us and what used to be a drone bounced and fell in pieces on the wide concrete pathway.

"What the fuck!" Helen said as she half crouched defensively.

"Sorry Sir, really sorry." A spotty teenager shouted as he ran towards us, gathered quickly all the remains and was about to sprint off with his evidence.

"Justin! Say sorry, to the lady."

The young guy stood without releasing his precious cargo. He was wearing a denim jacket and one of those floral fashionable shirts that Rayfinger must have bought at a job lot. He had bleached hair and eyes so blue you could see as far as Finland.

"Sorry, lady. "He was about as sorry as Nero. While he was about to make his escape he dropped one of the landing legs. I bent to pick it up but his reaction was like greased lightning.

"It's alright Sir, it's alright." He said insistently and nearly elbowed me out of the way to retrieve it. He secured his precious cargo and then fixed me with an unnerving gaze.

"I like your wheels." He said.

"Thanks." I said.

"Yes. Red suits the Mercedes."

"Sure," I said.

"The four cylinder doesn't depreciate as much as the V6. Good decision." He said. His voice and his totally still body seemed to be out of sync.

"Thanks."

Pastor Tommy patted him lightly on the shoulder. "Justin is blessed. Blessed with a touch of the old technical genius."

Justin looked at Tommy, unblinking. "I'm very competent but I'm not a genius." It was a statement of fact but the broken drone in his hands didn't auger well.

Pastor Tommy watched him retreating to the hanger until Tammy tugged his shirt and clapped his hands. "Well, let's get this show on the road." And it was done, faster than Perry's Circus.

We walked into the administration block. It was a tale of two cities. The interior was laid out in squirrel tight corrals either side of a long aisle to a room at the end. It was like a Victorian shoe factory which might have accounted for the average age of the youngsters crouched over laptops. None of them actually looked up but you could somehow tell that beady little eyes were following every step taken by their leader and his mystery visitors.

"Doing their school homework?" Helen asked.

Tammy Rayfinger turned and gave her the benefit of a sunny apple pie smile. "Whatever it is honey, they're doing it for the Lord."

There was an office door at the end of the aisle. There was a small sign on the glass. KNOCK AND IT SHALL BE OPENED (Matthew 7: 7-8) I assumed it was something that passed as an in-house joke.

"Just stay behind and see what those young kids are doing." I whispered to Helen. "Screenshots if you do it discreetly."

"Ahh, our little home away from home." Pastor Rayfinger announced. If it was like his home, that must have been a Spanish castle. A heavy dark oak dining table would have seated twenty or more people even with the solid wood and fabric chairs in place. The windows were framed by thick burgundy curtains that could have been picked up from an abandoned cinema. On the paneled blackwood walls were framed portraits of young people and happy grandparents. The actual parents had probably been kidnapped gratefully by aliens.

The late afternoon light picked out two men in dark suits standing behind their chairs like undertakers at a funeral. At the far end was a middle age woman who, on first glance at her conservative cardigan and ruffled shirt, could have carried the coffin. In fact the whole place had a funereal air that either connected you to God or made you uneasy, depending on your point of view.

On closer inspection one of the trio was probably in his late teens or he'd been locked up in a computer mainframe for his developing years. His thin neck left a lot of room for his white shirt and tie and you could tell his horn rim glasses were not retro.

The other one was a meatier version of the young one but he still sported the same close hair-cut and white soft hands which he extended forcefully.

"Meet the *Coming Now* Brains Trust," Pastor Rayfinger said. I did not doubt him but there was something a bit grittier about the older man as if he could explode suddenly and hurl us all into eternity.

"Brother Lester Underwood." The oldest one said and pumped

my hand like Donald Trump's grandfather. His accent was Transatlantic with an Aussie twang hiding behind it. He had blue eyes that looked through you as if he was watching for assassins behind you. What was even more disconcerting was the fact that his head and shoulders moved as one.

Despite the first impression, the woman was amiable. I knew that because she bounded around the table, which would have taken a slow runner close to an hour, and smiled like a librarian who has just discovered how the Dewey system works. She had long fingers and a soft handshake, which came as a surprise after that burst of athleticism. Unlike Tammy she wore no make-up at all except her hair was dyed a strange grey colour as if she was slowly being dragged into girl's make-up land. "Rachael Overton. Archives." She said briskly.

"And Lieutenant Marcus Gormley, our Communications Systems Officer. He handles the Big Friend." He said indicating the youngest one who merely nodded. It wasn't friendly but I guessed soon enough that we weren't going to be best friends.

"Big Friend?" I said.

"The personal data base." Marcus Gormley said evenly into his laptop. He didn't look at me. *From now on mate, you are not going to be Marcus Gormley but Lieutenant Squeaky (Army Reserves).*

From the moment we walked into the Spanish room, Pastor Tommy was in his element. He gestured for all of us to be seated, clapped his hands and held out his long arms. It took a moment for me to realise that we were all going to hold hands and pray. I looked at Robert who was willing himself onto another planet. Tammy took my other hand and held so tight I could feel the sparkling rocks on her fingers. Pastor Tommy closed his eyes but I took a furtive look at Tammy who was so close I could see the cracks in the mascara and the thin penciled lipstick line. She opened her eyes for a moment and pursed her lips as Tommy rolled out the prayer.

"Lord Jesus, today we ask for your blessing and the benefit of your wisdom. Strengthen our mind and every sinew as we wrestle with those that seek to do us harm and lead us into very bad ways. We ask that we can be pilgrims on that journey to kindness, humility and charity. Amen."

"Amen." I said but Brother Lester Underwood beat me to it.

Pastor Tommy clapped his hands again and we all sat. He looked around. "Well, let's open that kimono again and see how the flag flutters."

"Yep, let's see how it flutters" I repeated and avoided the amusement in Robert's eyes.

"Well it's like this." Tommy said, "We're nearly out of time and we need to start this day at top speed." Then he looked straight at me. "That's why we paid you up front."

"Appreciated." I said and really meant it.

Tommy flicked a remote control and the velvet curtain closed and a screen lowered. On the screen was our first attempt or I should say, Robert's first attempt at the *Coming Now* brochure designed for letter boxing and cinema adverts. There was a full screen of the Rayfinger family looking like the Von Trapp family in their retro simple goodness. Behind them a wheat field shimmered in the summer heat.

"Now I like what Team Kennedy did with this. Very good. But big problem. We don't want wheat-fields." Tommy said biblically.

Robert bent his neck and mumbled like he had been hit by a buffalo. He recovered himself and lifted one eyebrow as if he were assisting Tommy after a bad fall. "You want lucerne, perhaps?"

"Lucerne is green." The voice came from the young nerd who did not look up as he tapped away at his lap-top. It was a firm statement but the voice had the squeaky timbre that would have got him bullied at school. I was already backing the bullies.

"Well, we can change it to oats." Robert said with a slight sigh.

"It should be lucerne. That's better for soil fertility." Lieutenant Squeaky said again.

"The yellow wheat looks more dramatic." Robert said evenly.

I remembered the Third Rule of Advertising which says the client must have an early win. "Easy peasy, Robert. We can change that. Next."

"RAR." Tommy said.

"RAR?"

"It's our numbers and congregation," Lieutenant Squeaky affirmed then explained as if to a child, "RAR. Resources and Reach. How many members we can persuade to devote."

Robert intervened. His cleared his throat. "Of the sixty thousand in your congregation across the country how many could...?"

"Seventy two thousand," Lieutenant Squeaky interrupted, "And almost all would be prepared to devote."

There is a school somewhere in Middle America where they churned out devotees like Squeaky. Those with lower grades opt to be serial killers.

Tommy flicked to the next slide. There was a table that was subdivided into goals and time lines. It was based on the questions we had already sent to Team Coming Now. "Now, I wanna take issue with your suggested time line." Tommy said.

"Like?" I asked.

"Like the goal of Prime Minister. You say, it's not possible under three years. I'm gonna call you out on that one."

"We've already got a Christian Prime Minister who thinks he's been touched by a miracle from above. Is he gonna choke on a democracy sausage? Three years is a minimum." I said but that didn't go down well except for Rachael Overton who brought her long fingers to her mouth cover her grin. Mrs. Overton obviously loved a touch of naughtiness.

Tammy tapped her fingers twice on the table.

"I think what Tommy means is that we have to make things happen, not wait for...circumstances." She tried to make it sound just a suggestion, laden with honey.

I shrugged. "The impossible takes a little longer but it can be done. Let's shorten that time frame and we get to make you PM within two years and...as Tammy says, we proactively change...the circumstances." It was total bullshit but if they wanted lucerne instead of wheat or to make Hobart the capital of Australia we were happy to devise a strategy and tie pink ribbons around it.

I looked at the table again. "But the first step is to get the 30 or so people in the Liberal Party who do the pre-selections to actually make you their candidate for the seat. Then we have got to get you elected, then your other elected Liberal colleagues have to choose you over Scott Morrison. A few steps there on the way. But, you'll need to start with the power brokers in the Liberal Party in Tassie."

"Already done." Tommy said firmly. I had some doubts about that but *Coming Now* was full of surprises.

"Then work out how you get your future Parliamentary colleagues on side."

"Done."

"Then work out how you win over the public who aren't members of your congregation."

"Done."

"Then work out why you need us." I said. There was only one person in the room who realised that was both a joke and a test; Rachael Overton, who tapped in Tommy's promises then relaxed in the straight back position they taught in the old typing classes. She looked like her role in life was fixing up messes left by blowhards and egomaniacs; all in a day's work.

I looked at Tommy carefully, trying to find evidence of delusion. No delusion, nothing but the kind of angelic toothy certainty already trademarked by the Prime Minister and thousands of marketing executives in glass towers.

Tommy nodded and Marcus Gormley aka Lieutenant Squeaky got up, bringing a large bound dossier and ostentatiously placed it in front of me. On closer inspection, he was older than he looked from across the air-strip sized table. There were fine lines around his thin lips and his hair had a touch of grey around the short sideburns. He was the type who would have reported you to the school principal and felt good about it.

"The SWOT analysis. Strengths and weaknesses of us and our competitors," Lieutenant Squeaky said. "A SWOT analysis is…"

"I know what a SWOT is." I said tersely.

Tommy leaned over and tapped the dossier, "Brother Underwood has done a lot of flag fluttering on this one. We wanna have you guys look through it. Identify our potential weaknesses. How are competitors and the media gonna attack us? I want you guys to imagine you are our enemies. What would you say about us? Then, we need your ideas on the counter-attack. Knock 'em for a six, pow!" He threw his big fist in the air like a prize fighter or full-back.

"Pow!" I said. It was a strange world in that dimly lit velvet Spanish bunker. I had a sudden urge to call for more light or whatever it was that Christian martyrs called out when they got burnt at the stake. Team *Coming Now* was a weird bunch of cats but it was still hard to tell whether they were unstoppable because they were nuts or whether they were just nuts. The five hundred grand that sat comfortably in our bank account did help my cogitation, though.

There was a knock at the door and Helen came in apologetically, tip-toeing like a deer to a seat that Mrs.Overton pointed to, friendly woman to woman. Helen slid into her seat. The high back of the chair made her look like the first female Pope. She slipped me a very meaningful glance and moved her head ever so slightly as if she had seen something extra-ordinary.

Pastor Tommy was on a roll. "Look, let me throw open our kimono again. *Coming Now* is a big organization and you are part of a team. We got demographic technicians" He pointed at Lieutenant Squeaky who fixed me with a satisfied unblinking gaze. "We got IT specialists, administrative geniuses like Brother Underwood and Mrs. Overton, we've got singers and musicians like Dennis Cyberg...we got..."

Tammy leaned towards her husband and gently corrected him. "Well we *had* Dennis Cyberg, didn't we Tommy? But the, uh, younger ones connect better with people who are not overtly mature like Dennis so, we now have music artists who are more...up with the times." She looked to me then to Helen as if we would understand. "You see. Dennis was just wonderful but he was a little overtly mature for our younger members." I had seen Dennis Cyberg advertised on those TV ads where slightly rotund old stars croon to badly dubbed back recordings.

Tommy shrugged apologetically. "Yeah, guys like Dennis, you know, were great once...but..."

"Yep." I said. "But they get overtly mature."

"So, archive Mr. Cyberg's videos." Rachael Overton said evenly and made a note on her laptop consigning the overtly mature crooner to the history bin.

Tommy nodded and continued his final message for the day. "Yep. But the point I was originally making is that *Coming Now* is big and we got a lot of players who make it purr like a Cadillac and you are part of that team. Team *Coming Now*."

"Glad to hear that. Part of Team *Coming Now*." I repeated for the benefit of my own po-faced team.

FIVE

First dawn

As we drove away we could hear the voices of a young choir across at the school singing a teenage version of Christian rock with all the requisite drums and guitars and earnest lyrics. Pastor Tommy and Tammy stood waving at our rear vision mirror.

"You would not believe it. This *Coming Now* is bigger than Ben Hur. You know what those young screen jockeys were doing? Well, they were doing lots of things but here's some." Helen said.

Robert sniffed. "They were practicing to be obnoxious?"

Helen ignored him. "Half of them were organizing deliveries for bibles and that type of crap but the other half were taking orders for events, like concerts. One girl was actually tracking a delivery truck which timed the minutes between deliveries and the number of parcels delivered and it kept asking the drivers to tap in when they were late, you know, not making the schedule. Weird. And then they were organizing street stalls. Like sausage sizzles and raffles at sporting events and outside hardware stores."

"You'd expect that." I said.

"No they had 112 of those sausage sizzles lined up. I saw the schedule. One hundred and twelve bloody sausage sizzles. Then they had CDs, videos and all that online delivery stuff like food and coffee and clothing. The order lists were big, big. "

I was thinking about 112 sausage sizzles and all the methane. "It'd take a lot of sausage sizzles just to pay our fees. So what do they actually do to turn over all that dough? Robert. How much did you say was going through their books, on your estimate?"

Robert opened his laptop.

"Roughly?" I said.

"Well, approximately $150 plus million if they all tithe."

"Tithe?" Helen asked.

"Each member of the congregation pays ten percent of their income to the Church. That's probably thirty thousand adults multiplied by an average of five thousand dollars. That's one hundred and fifty million. That and all that commercial activity you saw would come to a lot more. All tax free because they *are* a religious institution. They also get capital and other grants from governments for their schools."

We were crossing the Bridgewater Bridge, a strange name that never failed to amuse me which shows that, when it comes to jokes, oldies but goodies will be eternal. Wild ducks and black swans were already resting on the upriver side of the bridge. The early evening light captured the yellow grasses of early summer glowing on the bare hills, leaving clear outlines of isolated gums on their rounded summits. Soon enough autumn would come and the poplars in the nearby Derwent Valley would turn their leaves and, like migrating birds, the retreats from long week-ends and beach shacks would slowly begin.

"Look, *Coming Now* is bigger than we think and, driven. Keep digging you two and I'll give Dinny Dinham a ring. "

"Your favourite detective." Helen smiled.

"I avoid him like the plague."

"Until you need him." She smiled.

"Well, we're gonna need him now because I don't think we have the full story about *Coming Now*. Not by a long way."

"When do we do the real work for these jokers? I would have thought that it's a bit late to spend time doing a search on them now" Helen was only half serious.

"When we find out who we are actually working for. That's when we really commit." I said.

My phone rang. It was Charlotte, my ex-wife.

"Your timing is impeccable." I said.

"Are you alone?"

"I've been alone all my life."

"Yes, I can testify to that. But you've always been a good father."

"Charlotte, I'm driving. You're on voice over. Can I call you back?"

"But you never do. This is just a quick one."

I could see Helen looking vaguely out of the window as if the thistles and road side gravel had suddenly become Van Gogh's sun flowers.

"How's Evan?" I said. Evan was Charlotte's wealthy husband who seemed to sit on every board in Melbourne, or at least the ones that paid well.

"Don't be diversionary."

"Oh I won't be diversionary. So, what is this about?

"Well, we've just got some wonderful news."

"And that would be?"

"Daisy's been accepted for China."

"I thought she goes to Geelong Grammar?"

"Very funny. The school is going to China. I emailed you about it."

Helen and Robert were enjoying the road side views so much that they were breaking out into infectious grins. Even they knew where my police inspector ex-wife was taking the interrogation.

"And you want me to pay for" I said. It wasn't a question.

"That would be really helpful."

43

"Charlie,"

"Don't call me that. So you won't do it?"

"Charlotte. In fifteen years you have called me ten or so times and every single time you have asked for private school fees or world trips."

"Only for the children." Her voice suddenly became very court room. "Is it because you oppose private schools? Just on principle."

"Yes. It's because they allow some lucky kids to get the jump on others."

"That is the point, to give your flesh and blood the advantages... it's also about the values they get as well."

I slowed down to allow a large painted mini-van to cut in front of me. Amongst the graffiti on the back doors was *All Property is Theft but You Can Hire This*. Marxist thought had finally reached Hobart. "Charlotte. Charlotte, are you still there? The phone keeps cutting out."

"Fuck you!" Charlotte said and hung up.

I looked at my grinning colleagues. "Not a bloody word!"

We had just crossed the bridge when Robert shouted, *stop* and I quickly pulled over to the curb and gave the thumbs up to the other road users who honked their horns and flashed their lights.

"What the hell is this, Robert?"

"So sorry, so sorry. It's the light, the water and the swans. I'm awfully sorry but this can't wait." He opened the door and nearly became a badge on the bonnet of a Landcruiser that repeated the horn blaring dose. What kind of people go out of their way to install the Colonel Bogey March on their horn circuits?

Robert was already half way up the causeway, crouching low to take shots with his precious Hasselblad. He was sharp and nimble which must have been a handy asset when taking photographs of hunting lions and stampeding wildebeest.

"He's a fanatic." Helen sighed.

"Speaking of that, I don't trust Tommy Rayfinger to actually do the job on his own. I want you to find out who the Liberal Party pre-selectors are. Who owns them? Like, who are the power brokers that influence how they vote."

"What are pre-selectors when they're at home?"

"Jeez. Good help's hard to find nowadays. The preselection panel in the Lyons electorate are chosen by their local branches and they make the final decision about who will be the Liberal Party's candidate for Lyons. The State Executive only intervenes if a pre-selected candidate stuffs up big time. But these panels are usually heavily influenced by party heavies."

"Give me a name."

"Start with Senator Eric Abetz. He pulls a lot of strings. Then go to the State Director and,"

"Paddy. I have never done any work for a political party."

"I've never organised a Tupperware party or fought in the Middle East so we all start somewhere. Seriously. If I contact them, they'll put two and two together. Now, re who's who in the Liberal zoo, you'll find the relationship diagram on my computer. Read it and we can talk but make it quick. Then we'll need to take Pastor Tommy through the talking points when he chats to Abetz and the pre-selection panel members he influences. I'll send them over to you but the main thrust of Pastor Tommy's sales spiel runs like this. He's got the money and won't cost the Party a cent in the election campaign. Second, he's well known because of his football. Third is his data base of potential voters that the Liberals can plug into if they accept him as the candidate and fourth, there are all the volunteer campaigners and door knockers he can throw into the election. Anyway, you and Robert can put that together tomorrow and let me check it before we send it across to *Coming Now*. After that, we need to get onto the election campaign proper. That means we need the voting results in each election in every polling booth. How each of them voted over the last three Federal elections. Do it town by town, like Bothwell or Oatlands or Ross or Campbelltown or Sorell. Don't worry about the Labor vote. I'm looking at the micro parties, especially the ones that spent big money..."

"How's your brother Napoleon?"

"What?"

"Any more orders?" She was shaking her head, grinning wryly.

"None after the office closes. Where's that bloody Robert? Did a lion get him?"

Dinny Dinham was on a new health kick. No beers with the boys, no beers in front of the TV, no beers at the BBQ. And now, the big swim before work.

That is why I was invited to meet him at the Sandy Bay beach, one of the inner city sand strips that dared old blokes with wrinkles and budgie smugglers to try their luck in the threatening cold of the wider Derwent. I raised Lenny Lucic's problem with his drug dealing, gun toting chef.

"We want him moved on." I said.

Dinny was too intent on observing seagull social behaviour to look at me. "Can't do it." He said.

"Is there a reason?"

"Yes."

"So there's a reason?"

He turned to me. The salt water had given him the red eye look, like a seagull. "Jeez, you're like a broken record. Do I have to spell it out for you?"

"He's one of yours? Bloody hell! What am I gonna say to Lenny?"

"Nothing. You tell him nothing. But you give him this message. No sacking of that chef. He can break every plate in Hobart and you don't touch him. OK?" Then he laughed to himself. It was like a storm water drain, slow and in fits and spurts, and ended in a coughing fit.

"What?"

"Does he give you free meals?" And the drain starting laughing again at his own wit. It hadn't been a good morning's work so, when the coughing and spluttering finished, I raised the question of Pastor Rayfinger and the *Coming Now* team.

"Bullshit artist but he's loaded. Well, to put it in court terms, that *Coming Soon* outfit of his is loaded." Dinny said then added gratuitously, "Great name."

"Tell me about it. It's actually *Coming Now* not *Coming Soon*."

"Sounds like my Saturday nights." Dinny said ruefully then he relaxed and leant back on the bench like he was on the French Riviera. He was in his speedos and had a wet towel draped around his neck. It was still a chilly dawn and Dinny's physical condition and the weather was the worst advert for physical exercise I'd ever seen, apart from those Japanese TV shows where the competitors get carted round on their bums to see who could withstand the most pain.

"Well, he says he lived in Bridgewater or Green Point in a Housing Commission rented home." Dinny said.

"Yeah. From humble beginnings."

"Bullshit! His old man bought up a lot of those places when the Government in its wisdom sold them off. Tommy Rayfinger lived there for a while so he could collect the rent and keep an eye out for the battlers that couldn't meet their mortgages. Then they'd make the poor buggers an offer they couldn't refuse. The old man is also a silent partner in a debt collection agency and three real estate agencies. He's bloody loaded but I tell you what, he's got the first penny he ever made. Humble bloody beginnings! Jeez, give me a break."

There were other brave souls out there slowly swimming across the face of the beach. It seemed like a good day to enjoy the exercise, vicariously through other people. But you had to admit that, at that time of the day there was a fair bit of serenity floating around, undisturbed by traffic or disaster stories on the morning radio.

Dinny drew a dose of sea water up into his nostrils.

"Dinny, do you have to do that?"

"Good for the tubes mate. Why all the questions about Tommy Rayfinger? He a client of yours?"

"Yep."

"Thought you'd check out your clients before you took their dough. You going bad or something?"

"Things get tight from time to time."

"You know you ought to buy a lot of those regional newspapers and throw-aways, like your competitors did. They got,"

"I know what they've got!"

"Touchy! Must be a little soft spot there."

"There bloody is! We were offered the chance to buy three of those regionals. Chicken feed and..."

"They give you a lot of political clout and..."

"Dinny, I bloody know. It's just that I didn't have the dough at the time."

"Could've flogged that car and all your fancy furniture."

"Dinny, you know me. I've got a rat pack mentality. I like bright things in my nest and I never get rid of them."

He worked on his other nostril. "Pathological, that's what you are. She want more money?"

"Yep, school trip to China."

"Jeez, you been divorced for fifteen years. And she's a cop? Stop feeling guilty. You're like one of those Cistern monks."

"Cistercian."

"What?"

"*Cistercian*...monks."

"That's what I said. Cistern".

We sat for a while and felt the new slowly increasing warmth on our faces. One of the cruise ships slid out into the wide river, its low pitched horns warning off the Wednesday yachties who were already leaning out into the light breeze. Dinny squinted and thought for a while.

"Follow the money."

"What?"

"Follow the money and the money is in real estate with every foreign bugger trying to buy up here in Tassie. And a lot of it isn't clean. Did the Reverend Tommy pay you up front?"

He hadn't looked at me.

"Yes. As a matter of fact I did get paid up front."

Dinny patted me on the leg or, more truthfully, put a full crab-grab on my knee. It was some kind of warning.

"Very wise."

SIX

Secret things

"This is Eric." Robert said and waited for my reaction.

Eric didn't look up or speak until he'd keyed some more programing language into the computer. I could see his body builder shoulders and thick neck before I saw the packet of Marella Jubes and a Coke bottle on one of our desks. Eric punched in a few more numbers and pressed print before he spun his chair and held out the open palm of his hand which I was expected to high five. I waited until he was about to withdraw his before I gingerly tapped back. I could see immediately that we were going to get along fine once Eric learned to speak English.

Both Robert and Helen were in the room. They were there to learn but a lot of that learning probably involved seeing how Eric and I were going to become the best of friends.

"Would you like Eric to walk you through what he's done so far?" Robert said and adjusted his cufflinks for the occasion.

The back of Eric's T-shirt said T.S.ELIOT, WHO DAT? Which proved he was literate.

"Your program's shit." Eric also proved he could speak. "Your inputs are in error whenever I want to drill down or print out email addresses."

"Good. Now we've got proof positive we should have spent more than the ten grand we splurged on programming." I said and didn't look at either Helen or Robert who had urged me to spend big and do it right the first time.

"Big Friend is bloody shit hot though. Wow, those guys know how to write programs and bring it all together. We're gonna love working for them"

"Great, Eric," I said and thought, you wouldn't like it at all and what's more you are never going to even cross the palatial doorsteps of *Coming Now* while I'm in charge. Putting technical geniuses in front of each other is a guaranteed social and political disaster.

"Just some house-keeping Eric. You work directly to Patrick Kennedy and Associates and invoice us direct."

"Whatever," said Eric from somewhere inside the computer.

"And what's your charge for each day?"

"Three thousand plus GST. You know you've got a 144 error in here?" He tapped the screen. He had inordinately small hands, an evolutionary outcome designed for texting I guessed.

"A 144? No I honestly never knew that. I must attend to it. Three grand. Isn't that over the odds by a thousand a day?"

"Got a company to run. We got twenty on the payroll."

"Oh, that's ok then. The other twenty could move here." I said to Eric's back.

"Nope. This place is a bit of a museum. Wouldn't like it."

"OK, Eric. Walk me through the lot."

Eric spun his chair around and I noticed his denim shorts on stocky hairy legs that ended at his sandals. Strangely, I was still trying to work out how old Eric was. My guess at that moment was somewhere between nine years old and forty. Nothing important but it helped to position ourselves in our respective centuries.

"Well. Point one. These *Coming Soon* dudes,"

"*Coming Now*." Helen said in an almost motherly way. Where she had come from, dealing with man boys would have been par for the course.

"Yeah. *Coming Now*. Well. They've got a data base that is impeccable," I liked his choice of *impeccable*. "Yep. That Big Friend is something special."

"You've been inside it?"

Eric looked surprised at my naivety. "Of course. It's not hard to breach. There's enough proprietary software to give us a few entry points."

"How can it be...*impeccable* if it's got holes in it?"

"Well, there are backdoors in all systems. Sometimes it's those Parliament idiots who pass laws that force companies like telcoes to build in backdoors to give cops and anti-terrorist dudes a chance to monitor bad guy behaviour. It's a joke. Cause that's exactly what the bad guys then use to get back in." He shook his head in disgust at the stupidity of our esteemed governments.

"OK. Can we improve on what Big Friend does, so we can help our clients, like *Coming Now*?"

"Improve? Do you really know much about..." He searched for a word, "Computers?"

I looked at Helen and Robert and was met with two straight faces that would have done justice to Solomon.

"Stuff all." I said.

Robert and Helen were of one mind. "Stuff all." They said simultaneously.

"OK. Lemmie walk you through. You know how personal data bases are built up? They're just lists with personal details added. Right?"

"Right." *Get to the point Eric.*

"Well, a lot of this is collected with your permission. You sign up for rewards in shops, phone companies, airlines, competitions, surveys on the phone, hire purchase, after-pay, Facebook, Google and all the social media and so on, and all that gets amalgamated and sold. It's actually sold on with your permission, all those details. But nobody reads the fine print."

"Eric. I know that. That's what we do for our clients but we do it within the Privacy Act."

Eric, for the first time, looked uncertain. "Yeah, the Privacy Act." As if I had said, *my great aunt's lavender bags.*

It was getting very close in that office. Four of us and those humming computers and modems could have been on a space ship. I remembered once reading about the computer billionaire Robert Mercer who was the genius who used his money and genius to help Donald Trump target the right voters and win an election without bothering to get more actual votes than Hillary Clinton. Mercer is reported to have said that the most wonderful feeling was to be sitting amongst his whirring and humming computer rooms in the early hours of the morning. Once I would have laughed. Nowadays, who was laughing?

"Eric. We know about the data bases that are collected with people's so called permission. What about the ones that are collected and used with everyone being in the dark?"

Eric turned his chair and slapped his tiny hands on his thighs. "Well, that's the question isn't it? There's local government rolls. They have the value of your house and so on. There's the electoral roll which has the name and address of every voter in the country. There's all that census data. There's real estate lists with really personal details on them. You know, I once saw my own little story on that list. Woo! Comanche time! You know what it said?"

I didn't want to know what real estate agents felt about Erik the Viking and his habits but there *was* something he could tell us about. "Eric. Now let's just assume. If a religious organization like...let's say *Coming Now*, was to get political. They would be entitled, if they ran a candidate, to access all those rolls and have them in electronic form. You know, the voter rolls, census data, the local government data base and those other ones if they got their hands on them."

"And they would be exempt from the Privacy Act because they are part of a political party or even could consider themselves to be a media organization. Right?" Helen said. She folded her arms, waiting for the answer. Eric shrugged.

"Don't know about that." He said blithely.

Helen persisted. "Eric. So, if all these were amalgamated, how close to the census groups could a letter or email go? I mean could you actually send a letter specifically designed to touch every interest of one individual. Could even be different from other people in the same house?"

"Of course. That's what the political parties are close to doing now. But they'll need Facebook and so on to do it because the Australian Bureau of Stats has purposely built in perturbation to make it more difficult. You see, when you micro-simulate..."

Helen turned to me. "Can we uh, talk outside?"

We stood in the corridor. Robert and Eric talked technical jargon inside but I could tell which one was doing the interrogation because with Robert he could pluck Wikipedia from your brain while you thought about your shopping lists.

"Jeez. It's close in there." She said, mock fanning herself. She was wearing a plain white T-shirt that seemed crisp and clean in comparisons with Eric's.

"And what is on your mind?"

"You haven't asked me that for, quite a while?"

"I don't like to intrude."

She nodded in the direction of the office where Robert was leaning over the computer as Eric took him into cyber world like a cave explorer to a tourist. Every now and then Robert said, uh, huh and it wasn't out of politeness.

"Well. You know, you may have been right to have forced us to work for *Coming Now*. I can tell you I bloody hated the idea."

"Hang on. Was I right or was I right?"

"You were right but for the wrong reason."

"I knew that was too good to last."

She laughed. Her snub nose always wrinkled and a little white space appeared momentarily on the end of it when she laughed. She wore her hair long today so that it fell over her T-shirt. Botticelli would have approved.

"You know, if we get possession of Big Friend and those new data bases, we will have a product that will put us back on top again. We can guarantee to our select clients a data base that pin points every individual in this country. Correct?" She said.

"Correct." I said.

"Is it legal?" She said.

"What's legal? I know a man that was jailed for just looking at his wife then he choked to death on gooseberry pie in jail. That's capital punishment and that's not legal."

She pushed me gently on the chest.

"So, that's yes?"

"I presume you and Robert have already discussed this? Which is why he's in there drilling Erik the Viking for more info? OK. I want Robert to work with you alongside Eric. Get what we want. Doesn't matter how many days. Well, at three grand a day, it does matter, but get what we need then lock him out for good and isolate everything on a separate network elsewhere. And..."

She laughed. "And?"

"And, for Christ's sake, get Donna to put a water jug in there each day and bring him healthy sandwiches. Coca Cola and chips! He'll never go the distance."

SEVEN

And the greatest of these is charity

Sunday evening and Helen and I were on our way to conduct another focus group in the Derwent Valley. Unlike other pollsters we meet the punters in their own homes and they invite friends who invite friends. It's more disorganised but, that way, people are a little more open with each other. On that day we were asking questions trying to find out whether being a pastor was going to handicap Tommy Rayfinger's election chances. If the focus groups were accurate, the punters weren't too keen on having a reverend gentleman in the Parliament.

"They need to look after their Church and leave it up to the politicians to look after us," seemed to just about sum it up. But being a Premiership footballer won Tommy enough browny points to compensate. We were still running these focus groups trying to find an angle that would help Tommy reach out beyond his religious flock for votes. There had to be a formula that worked beyond football.

We were waiting at the traffic lights near the Hobart Show Grounds where they were assembling more tents for the homeless that were the losers in Tassie's grab for millions of tourists and foreign University students.

A food van was parked outside the gates and volunteer workers were carting food trays into the communal area. Then came the big surprise. There was Robert Malahide in an apron carrying a tray of what looked like fruit juices and bread.

"It's that bloody Robert." I said. I was still a bit sore about him refusing to work on week-ends but, still, that would have put me in the same boat as half the bosses in the state.

Helen looked at me strangely. She was in her best tailored slacks and cream shirt, ready for the focus groups. "Yeah, does look a bit like him. Green light."

As we pulled away, I said again. "That *was* Robert."

"Watch the road."

On Monday morning I called Robert in.

"Close the door."

Robert looked stressed. "What have I done that's untoward?" He avoided my eyes and fiddled with one of the tiny Lalique glass deer pieces I had picked up in an op shop although it turned out to be the real thing. Well, it was the real thing until Robert broke its ear off by dropping it on the parquet floor.

"Oh dear. I seemed to have broken its ear. So sorry old man." He made a fantasy attempt to fix the pieces. "I'm awfully sorry. I didn't realise it was so delicate."

"Yeah, anything made in the 1930s gets a little brittle." I lied.

He settled himself in the chair waiting for the bad news. "So, what have I done wrong?"

"Well, it's what you've done right."

Robert stopped his Sergeant Wilson impersonation and looked relieved. "And what have I done that is correct?"

"Well, not to put too fine a point on it, a little birdy tells me you've been feeding the poor."

His features were totally impassive and I knew that he wasn't going to answer. I pushed a little harder.

"Mate, I saw you at the Showgrounds yesterday. In an apron, serving food to the homeless."

He sat up more severely and spoke with all the patience you use to speak to a six year old. Well, I'm told the middle classes do it that way. Then, a lot of others send their kids away to boarding school, which might say something about their patience.

"They are not THE homeless. They are homeless people," He said emphatically.

"And?"

"And you should not ask questions about my...uh...private life."

"Oh we have a private life have we?"

He looked quite impassive.

"Well, I had one...once."

I was intrigued. Robert was a closed book. He did his job well. The photography and graphics were brilliant. The content was always spot on. His technical skills with Facebook and the other social media was red hot; far more adept and smarter than some of the young nerds we used to employ.

He sat there that day with a face set as beatifically as Mother Theresa, waiting me out.

"Robert. I'm just curious." I began.

"You have never shown the remotest interest in my private life before." He interrupted.

"True. Your private life is your private life but it's just weird that you keep your good works a secret. Honestly, I'm really interested. Why do you do that kind of charity work?"

He didn't move a muscle. "Because, I'm a Catholic."

"So is the Pope."

He lifted his eyebrows.

"I'm a Recusant Catholic. My whole family is."

"Ah, a Recusant Catholic. That explains it all." I lied.

He looked me squarely in the eye. The Eternity, Helen called it, looking at you and through you at the same time.

"To put it simply, the Recusants are the great old Catholic families who refused to recognise the Tudors and others who wanted to break with Rome. For them there was only one true religion but their loyalty to the Pope had consequences."

"Go on."

"Well, they became persecuted, a little inbred, a little isolated. Right down to modern times. Accept Pope John the Twenty Third's modernizing of the Church? Oh no way. The recusants are a very rigid lot. Much too overtly moral and obsessed with things like retaining the old Latin liturgy and the incense and the candles and the conversations with saints, that type of thing. Rigid. That's why I'm here in Australia." He paused, "Are you really…interested in this?"

"It's been a slow day at the office and I don't want to listen to all those recordings from the focus group, so," I pushed the intercom.

"Yes Mr. Kennedy."

"No calls for fifteen minutes."

"Yes Mr. Kennedy."

"Now Robert Malahide. Let's have the big G gossip. Did you have a castle and a priest hole?"

He seemed surprised at my vicarious questions. It was like I'd asked if his mother was an axe murderer.

"We had an…estate and, yes, it did have a priest hole."

I opened my laptop. "Name?"

"Minnie."

"Pardon?"

He smiled. When Robert actually smiled, rather than offering a kind of strangled grimace, it was like the sun had come out.

"Minnie," he repeated then, noticing my confusion, he added, "When we were children we called it Minnie because it was a priest hole. It got confused with a mouse hole." He smiled almost dreamily at the thought.

"No, I mean the name of the estate."

"Oh, Buckland House."

I Googled it which tried to tell me that Buckland House was in Tasmania. Smart phones, smart IT. Then, there it was. A seventeenth century Elizabethan pile of golden sandstone with more windows than Buckingham Palace. A row of oaks or elms led up a slight incline to the manor house. I would have sold the priest into slavery if he'd endangered that inheritance.

I turned the photo towards him. He nodded and had that dreamy look again.

"Yes. That's it. You know, one of the priests that my family hid was actually sent by the Pope to assassinate Queen Elizabeth. My grand-parents put a plaque outside the Priest hole to commemorate the event."

"I will never cross you."

He smiled. "Don't worry, my family, God bless their moral little hearts, wouldn't lift a finger in my defence. Too busy on their knees, in darkened chapels."

"Robert the Black-sheep?" I asked. "I can't see you bobbing and standing and kneeling and reciting Latin. Everyone's got a funny tribe I suppose."

He stopped smiling and began the Sergeant Wilson variations again. "Something like that. For the record, I don't bob and kneel and speak Latin, as you put it. And now, if you don't mind, I need to finish that electronic brochure for Pastor Rayfinger." He said the name as if the heretic preacher Tommy Rayfinger was responsible for every religious war of the last millennium.

"Why are you willing to work for the Rayfingers when it's pretty obvious you despise them?" I said.

"I don't despise them."

"Yes you do."

"Well, a little. I like my Christianity to care for everyone, not just the chosen smug few. Singing songs and clapping your way into a guaranteed heaven isn't the same as doing good works. So, I'll work for the Rayfingers and I'll use some of their money to house the homeless and a few other practical things."

"The Rayfinger Tax?"

He smiled. "Yes. I like that. The Rayfinger Tax."

He stood and adjusted his cuffs and shrugged to unrumpled his suit. For a man who sat at a desk all day he was in good nick as they say in the gyms. He turned at the door.

"For what it's worth, the Happy Clappers, as you call them, love their music and a good dose of ecstatic behaviour and Recusant Catholics like my dear family dwell in gloom. But they do have one thing in common, they will welcome a world catastrophe because it is God's judgement and they know they'll be saved. Just a thought."

"Just a thought." I said.

I waited until he left and then rang Donna.

"Donna."

"Yes, Mr. Kennedy?"

"Donna, could you write a cheque for a thousand bucks and post it to Loaves and Fishes? You know, the homeless charity?"

There was a pause. "From what account Mr. Kennedy?"

"From the donations to charity account."

"Mr. Kennedy. We don't have a charity account."

"Well, we do now."

"That's so good of you Mr. Kennedy. Mr. Malahide would really appreciate that."

"Donna, who said anything about Robert?"

There was another pause on the line. "Because he does all that kindly work for Loaves and Fishes and also the Salvation Army."

"Am I the last person round here to know when good works are being done?"

"Oh we don't want to bother you."

I thought, *next time I'll deduct his salary for breakages.*

EIGHT

One flesh

The *Coming Now* compound was like the MCG on Grand Final day. There were cars everywhere being directed by young people in fluorescent safety vests and plastic batons which glowed like Lightsabers from *Star Wars*. The crowd was mostly families with a lot of surprisingly well dressed teenagers; denim jackets, tailored jeans and carefully selected dresses. It was strangely quiet, like everyone was there with a single purpose in mind. The day was coming to an end and a wind had come up from the South bringing with it a few spots of rain and the scent of damp grass.

"Are they gonna handle snakes?" Helen said. A while ago she was worrying about crazies sending her strange messages and today she was taking the mickey out of snake handlers and religiosi who spoke in tongues.

"Behave yourself." I said.

Robert had begged off and I was happy to let him go, although the way he and Helen interacted often led to our more creative moments. And believe me, creative inspiration can get thin when, for a long time, we were paid to promote industries that made cities and countryside look like concrete bunkers or bombed fields.

We entered the auditorium which was already close to capacity, probably three thousand. There was hum of quiet conversation as technicians moved sound equipment around on the stage and adjusted the brightness of the massive screens that peered down overhead.

The young attendant in jeans and blue coloured T-shirts looked at our tickets. "Welcome, a really super welcome to Mrs. Troy and Mr Kennedy."

"Ms." Helen said firmly, "Ms Troy."

The young woman looked at us both for a second, perhaps looking for the section reserved for sinners then recovered her white teeth exposure. "Ms. Troy and Mr. Kennedy. God bless."

The whole stage was the same burgundy colour that we had encountered in the Spanish room but bunches of flowers and small pine trees in pots were placed strategically to the right and left to lighten the atmosphere.

Soon, the auditorium was packed and the ushers, dressed in the same uniform of jeans and blue T-shirts closed the doors behind us. A choir of about thirty people of all ages immediately filed onto the stage and stood without conversation, looking straight ahead as if deep in thought. Their satin red college gowns looked like a bloody massacre.

There was then total silence for a minute or so. No music, no visuals on the screen bar one line of text. BEHOLD THE LAMB OF GOD.

Suddenly a tall man dressed in jeans and a navy blue jacket and pearly white shirt strode onto the stage. It was Pastor Tommy Rayfinger in all his glory. He walked purposely to the front of the stage. No introductions, no music. Straight to the sermon delivered in that Charlton Heston voice but, in that auditorium, it was strangely intimate and commanding.

"Friends, I met a man today. One of our congregation. A family man who I would bet, if I was a betting man, he is among the Chosen.

Yes. Chosen although none of will know that we are chosen until that day when everything and everyone will be judged. When our fight with the Devil and all his grimy fearsome warriors will be a battle for our eternities. A fierce battle that will rage street by street, park by park and into our own homes and our hearts.

Yes, that good man said to me. Pastor Tommy, he said to me. If it's harder for a rich man to get into heaven than a camel to get through the eye of a needle, then a lot of our congregation are going to hell. Even you Pastor drive a big flash SUV and you've got a lovely place in the country. Is it gonna be easy for you to get into heaven?

I said, brother, you don't know how much fuel that Land Cruiser burns up. It keeps me poor so I'm gonna get in." He paused for the mandatory laughter which came almost gratefully.

"You know. Seriously, folks. It isn't ever gonna be easy for anybody. Not for you or you or you; not for me and my saintly wife Tammy. Not easy. "He paused and walked a little then suddenly turned. Pastor Tommy may have looked like a dreaming dork when we first met him in my office but this was his world and he was loving it.

"So, this brother, this good, good man. I looked him in the eyes and I said no-one knows who's gonna get into that glory place called heaven. But, I said, brother, it's not a sin to be comfortable, it's not a sin to love your family so much that you are going to make them comfortable even prosperous. It is not a sin to want to make your family and your friends safe. Having a good safe car is a way of honouring and protecting your family."

He stopped and pointed at a woman in the front row. "You sister, my dear friend. You know it don't you? Working hard, doing it without governments, doing it without unions and charity. That's a way of honouring your loved ones and you know, it's your way of honouring Jesus.

I'm telling you. As sure as the Day of Judgement is coming, yes it's coming, when the lucky ones walk into their home at the end of the day and your wife is there and she's made herself as pretty as she can and your kids are there just kicking a football in the backyard or just doing their homework, and that's a miracle." He paused for a moment to allow that human touch to percolate around the auditorium. "And you're walking in and giving her a hug you can say to yourself, I have honoured my family, those I love and I am honouring the Lord Jesus, our Saviour."

He strolled across the stage, totally in control of the audience. There was a cough or two but it was all in Pastor Tommy's hands. Then he walked to the front of the stage and a familiar young woman, impeccably blonde but homely, brought something to him in both outstretched hands. Tommy stood silent for a moment then beckoned one of the roaming camera women to come forward to capture what he held in his hand. It was a small glass case about the size of a cigarette packet. The image was very clear as it was projected onto the overhead screens. Tommy turned the case reverently so that you could see the fragment on which Greek letters were written. There was a hush as if the audience knew what was coming.

"You know what this is? Believe me, you want to know. This is...but lemmie tell you first how I got it, praise the Lord. When I was in Bible College a man called me. We attended the same church together but he was dying, he was passing over. Lemmie tell you about this man. He was a true bible scholar. He could speak seven languages and he had spent most of his life in the Holy Land and at Oxford, England. That's where he worked as a Professor of Archaeology. Seven languages! My wife, Tammy, reckons I can't even speak one, bless her sense of humour." He waited for the laughter which duly came as if canned for that moment. "He was ailing badly so I drove through the night because, you know passing over is a glorious event and I wanted to be there when he passed. Yes glorious!

And when I got there he called me forward. He had his loving family around him and wouldn't we all want that when we pass over? He called me forward and he pressed this into my hands and said take this in remembrance of me. This, he said, is the oldest known fragment of the New Testament. Mark, yes, the word of God passed down direct, yes, direct from Mark to this scholar and now, two thousand years later, it is here for you to see with your own eyes. Look. Look and glory. Come, look. This is the Breath of God. Given to us. The Breath of God."

There was a visible intake of breath as Tommy lifted the glass case in both hands. Holding it aloft, he began a long slow prowl back and forth across the stage whispering "the *word of God, the breath of God*. Here today for you and you and you and you." He pointed it in different directions so that the reflected light alternated like a tiny lighthouse.

"Yes, the word of Mark passed down in physical form to us. And you know what Mark says? I'll tell you what he says. It says, *honour your family. Honour your family. A man and a women are one flesh. Help the little children. You are here for that.* That's what it says. That's Mark speaking direct to you and me over two thousand years, from then on to the End Times. The Day of Judgement. Do not, do not ask for who the bell tolls. That's a dumb, dumb question. Bells are tolling everywhere and when it comes, when the Rapture comes and the godly rise. Your loved ones, your mothers, your fathers, your passed friends and relatives. They are gonna rise with you. Can you hear it? The breath of God. Look at it. Can you hear it? Hear it. Listen."

Tommy was leaning over the edge of the stage and there was silence. His voice was soft as he beckoned the audience. Then he held out both hands and swayed. "Can you hear it? Come. Come forward. Come forward. The breath of God."

The audience swayed and, one after the other, pockets of the crowd started to wave their arms overhead and others came forward to the stage front where they were met by men and women dressed in sombre suits. The attendants touched each newcomer on the forehead. Soon the front was full and the choir broke into song, this time Christian Rock aimed at teenagers. *Teenage pain and suffering and love that outfit and Jesus saves and we dress our best for Jesus and he loves us for it.*

As the choir sang, young people in jeans and smart leather or denim jackets emerged from the wings, like may flies in spring, until they filled the stage. A door had been opened somewhere which allowed a chilling breeze to penetrate the hall and riffle the curtains. The choir paused as *Pastor Tommy gave it his best full back, last minute interception and the crowd rose to its feet and knew they were in communion with a real man for real people who was going to keep them safe no matter how often the attackers went into their forward line.*

"Can you hear it? Coming now. Happiness and honour or pain and suffering. All, coming now. Happiness and honour or eternal pain and suffering. What will you choose?"

NINE

Smelling the battle far off

Saturday morning. We were in Primrose Sands, an isolated beach hamlet of a thousand people, perched on a series of hills, rustic fibro shacks painted in strange combinations of blues and greens. Recent invaders have built more expensive beige and grey homes from the Beige and Grey Catalogue but they still got the same million dollar views over the clear blue sea towards Mt. Wellington, Bruny Island to the South West and the forests of Tasman Peninsular tucked behind the islands. At different times of the year, whales and dolphins come into the Bay and verandas would be full as the locals and weekend shackies oohed and arghed at the leaping beauties. Then the whales and dolphins would suddenly be gone and the only fish around would be a few sharks out in the channel and flat head or squid destined for the gas barbeques which crouched on balconies like culinary ships of war. This was thongs, bare feet and baggy shorts territory where man fights the sea and man always wins.

We'd been to Sorell where Tommy was showing Helen and me the planned area for a new package delivery centre for which *Coming Now* was seeking development approval. Co-incidentally, like the *Coming Now* HQ in Brighton, the planned centre was in the electorate of Lyons.

"Lots of jobs in hungry country towns." Tommy had said proudly.

"Packing hubs delivering on time. The highways of the future. Did you know that the average package gets dropped or damaged sixteen times in the last kilometre?"

"I didn't know that," Helen said, straight faced. If we'd both been smart we would have understood the real plan behind the Sorell venture but we found out soon enough. In the meantime Tommy regaled us with stories about the way the geniuses at *Coming Now* could tap into the internet and market everything from groceries to bibles or Christmas gifts or votes.

"Yessir. We got data bases that would take your hair off and peer inside your brain, and your heart. That's how we're gonna win this campaign. Good, modern business technology and targeted marketing. You know, that's what the Lord Jesus wanted. Don't hide your talents, use the modern technologies to invest in your personal future."

"Jesus said grab new technology? Did he really?" Helen said. "She tapped her iPhone and got onto the Facebook Page of a few small towns near us. "OK Pastor, here we go. The Facebook page for the Primrose Sands and Connelly's Marsh community. Have a look at what Tracey and Nadine say about life in general and that bloody dog that's always on the loose. Wow! They don't muck about. Paddy, you've got a shack down there at Primmie haven't you? Maybe you could intro the Pastor down there."

Thank you Helen for sharing my secret place with a client that we were always on the edge of ditching. Thank you very much.

It was an irritating kind of day, everyone tip-toeing like a thief around personal issues and business issues. And right now the big problem was the over-reliance that the *Coming Now* team were placing on new technologies and social media to help them actually avoid meeting voters. They'd done ok chatting up the conservative pre-selectors, *oh yes, abortion and drugs are bad and pornography worse* but meeting ordinary voters out there was another matter. They were breaking Advertising Rule Number Four. *Technology or biology? In a crunch, always choose biology.*

It was a crisis that only Tommy could solve. He was the candidate. He needed to direct his funereal advisors to leave their computer screens and revival meetings and step outside the Bible Bubble. So, to Primrose Sands in Voterland the pilgrims went.

I made Tommy stand on the side of the road as utes and Four Wheel Drives headed down to the launching ramp at Gipsy Bay. It was like Pitt Street for blokes, women and children by invitation only. Blokes, in Richmond footy caps and T-shirts, parking trailers with boats on them, centimetre perfect. Blokes incongruously standing ready at the wheel of boats on moving trailers, Captain Cooks and Baudins searching for another sea to conquer or at least as far as Sloping Island over there. *I will provide.* Nissan Navara N-TREK Warrior, Amaroks, Yamahas 175, Ford Ranger Wildtrak X, Toyota Rugged X, Toyota Klugers for hunting lions in Safari Parks, Pajero V8s not to be confused with the Decimator 357 and the Getoutatheway V8 Gutfinder, proving your kids didn't need a fancy University degree to catch the good life every weekend.

"Great views. Look out there. Those islands and the mountains beyond. It makes you glad to be alive." Tommy said. "Where's your place?"

"Around the corner." I said. I kept my holiday shack a total secret but today I was on a mission to convert Tommy Rayfinger and his Team *Coming Now.* Sure as hell there'd be no beers and fish and steaks on the balcony, just Pastor Tommy getting a few lessons in meeting and greeting. We got in Tommy's 4WD, Tommy gunned the engine and we soon pulled up in front of my shack perched up on its piers for a better view of the islands and Norfolk Bay.

Tommy leaned out the window. "Which place is yours? Don't tell me, don't tell me. It's that one, the modern one with the big glass and garage. I like it. Got lots of class."

"Nope it's the one that was last painted in 1948 and it leaks and the trees are crying out for water. That one. But the tinnie works and the outboard motor gets me home each time."

"Oh," Tommy said. He was sympathetic but puzzled. I remembered his sermon about honouring your family by giving them a comfortable life and I knew then I wasn't going to heaven and there were a lot of others in Primrose Sands that were also going to miss out too.

"See my neighbour Trevor's house?" I pointed at a humble house with a campervan in the yard, "Well he brings me fish when he's been out there. He's got a ride-on mower. Mows the grass for his neighbours. He and his mate Bill next door felled a dangerous tree for me. Just for a slab, which was only symbolic"

"Slab?" Tommy was confused.

"Slab of beer. Carton of beer." I said. "And they have something to do with the Country and Western Round-Up every February. Good blokes. Helping their neighbours. Get it? Now, let's go up the road to the Rissole."

"The Rissole?"

"The RSL. Returned Services League Club." Helen said.

The RSL was quiet but a few families and the regulars were tucking into their twenty dollar parmigianas and there was a BBQ outside. It was that late summer period when football had not begun seriously and the cricket had finished. Women were finally getting their husbands' complete attention.

The Primrose Sands RSL is straight out of the RSL architectural handbook with the usual decommissioned artillery piece pointing aimlessly at enemies that would never turn up, a well-kept flag outside, honour boards for the fallen, like Eddie Burroughs or Vic Imlach every Saturday night, the football tipping board and a courtesy bus to take home the veterans. And the usual notice at the entrance; *no singlets and thongs.*

"Where's my flat-head, Dino?" I said to Dino Imlach.

"Get in line mate. I'm real popular now that Big Kev holed his tinny." Dino shifted on the bar stool to make way for our party. "Who's your big streak mate? Looks like Tommy Rayfinger that played fullback for St. Kilda."

Tommy nodded at me and was standing there with his hand half outstretched.

"Yeah, bloody Rayfinger" Dino said, not noticing "Got religion then left us in the lurch."

"Fires going to be alright this year?" I said.

Mary the barmaid put a beer in front of me and waited for the others to order. "Would have been all right if the Greenies had let 'em back-burn." There was no question of argument. Never argue when you're sober.

We collected our beers and sat at one of the tables with a view of the BBQ area. Outside, on the community caravan park, volunteers were converting an old shipping container into a stage and amenities block. There was lots of talk. *Obviously Kev was an idiot and Jacko was too lazy to breathe but old Billy just got on with it.*

Tommy sipped his fruit juice and stayed distant from our conversation. The Primrose Sands RSL was a long way from his Facebook followers or the happy clapping families that hung on his every word.

"You're quiet, Pastor Rayfinger," Helen said. "A lot on your mind?" A mischievous eye glance that told me a lot. She was wearing a green low cut frock that showed her bare freckled arms and allowed her hair to cascade down her exposed back. It wasn't Sunday Church style but it was Helen saying a polite *stuff you* to our client, on behalf of all at Patrick Kennedy and Associates.

"Yes, a lot Helen." It was the first time Tommy had addressed her by name.

"Well Pastor. What do think? Are we ready to burst outside that Bible Bubble?" She said. From someone who once knew nothing about politics Helen was at least across rule number one, *you should always be the one that asks the questions.*

Tommy winced. "Do you have to call it that? Let me tell you, that little phrase Bible Bubble, it doesn't go down well with some of our team."

I drained my beer. Out in the caravan park, blokes in daggy shorts and T-shirts that were under great strain were sitting precariously on folding camp stools while their wives washed up or tried to turn the Jayco-Millard Sunseeker 77 Easy Rider campervan into a suburban home.

"Well Tommy. You pay us to give advice. Problem is, I'm detecting a lot of passive resistance from the *Coming Now* team. That is not good so, this afternoon, we need to sort it all out."

"Mano-a-mano." Tommy said, getting up and subjecting me to the *Look Down*. That's the trick that tall leaders pull when they want to show their shorter brethren who is number one. "You've got it. We can sort this out in a civilised honest way."

"Yep. Civilised exchange of viewpoints." I said.

"That's bullshit!" I said.

We were once again in the Spanish room at the *Coming Now* compound in Bagdad. The lights were on but at least the velvet red curtains were open and afternoon light was still seeping through the stained glass windows and the lower level clear glass. Pastor Tommy and the two funeral directors were there alongside Tammy who looked like she was about to pull a gun and shoot us all down. I noticed for some baroque reason that Lieutenant Squeaky (Reserves) wore no jacket like the others but his black tie and white short-sleeve shirt was a uniform of sorts. Miss Rachael Overton, the archivist, was there but she was wearing a mauve angora cardigan and pearls as if dressed for the occasion.

Tommy sat back in his high backed seat. "OK, gun fight time. You tell me why we can't come down hard on illegal immigrant queue jumpers and why we can't be pro-coal, like all the Liberal Party members?" It was a direct challenge and the two funeral directors, especially Lieutenant Squeaky were enjoying the action, hoping like hell that Tommy would blow me away.

"Can I have a whiteboard?" I said.

"A whiteboard?" Said Lieutenant Squeaky as if I'd asked for a stone wagon wheel.

"Yes, a whiteboard."

There was a series of mobile phone calls demanding a whiteboard. A whiteboard? What? A whiteboard? Yes. A whiteboard. Finally, Rachael Overton pulled out a phone and made a brisk but friendly call and remembered to say thank you.

Finally they found a whiteboard and two young acolytes in the *Coming Now* T-shirts and jeans set it up, with difficulty, as the legs kept retreating inside the main leg.

I wrote one word on the white-board. MORRISON.

Tommy gestured for more, turning his large hands over like a spin bowler.

I wrote 2019 under MORRISON then COAL, REFUGEES, CLIMATE CHANGE then DONE.

"Because Morrison is the PM and by the time you get to challenge him, those issues will be gone, kaput, the tide will be in. You don't want to be stranded out there on a drowned island when everyone of consequence, like PM Morrison, has adapted."

It was the right time for the second rate mate to the bully in the playground. Lieutenant arrived on time. "Refugees? You mean illegal undocumented arrivals. On that one, we have to stick to the official *Parliamentary Liberal Party* line." He said the words *Parliamentary Liberal Party* like *Ark of the Covenant* or *Day of Judgement*. I ignored him and directed my remarks at Pastor Tommy. But first I wrote on the whiteboard. HOUSES BURN DOWN.

"Look Tommy. Morrison has the Party in his hands because he's running an ultra-conservative agenda and he's going to win this election. But things are going to change. There's a drought and there are gonna be big fires in Australia this summer or next summer. When that happens the punters out there with their Turbo diesel utes and Four Wheel drives get burnt out and TV and mobile screens are going to talk about nothing but fires and drought. Now here's the thing. The same turbo diesel driving supporters of Morrison this time around are gonna go sour on him next time because he mislead them about climate change. That's right, the very ones he will use to win with this time are gonna turn on him when their houses burn down."

"Where's the evidence for that big inferno?" Tommy said.

"It's in the science."

"Yes. That's just Green propaganda..." Squeaky began.

"Can I talk to the organ grinder?" I asked. We had reached the classic state in every PR project where the client was comfortable on one side of the river and we were trying to build a bridge to the other, to the future. My old man Patrick was full of boring aphorisms but borrowing one of them saved time at moments like that.

Tommy gestured for Squeaky to stay out of it although I was surprised that the young bloke was allowed to intervene in the first place but maybe that was my age showing. Tammy meantime, pursed her brightly coloured lips and fiddled with the brocade that decorated her little girl dress. There was a slight tapping of her red painted fingernails.

"Look, "I said, "Think about it. You're not gonna be PM this week. So keep your head down and wait. Until then, say nothing about climate change until you're asked directly. But when you are asked you must be direct. You say something like, *we must be prepared. We need to prepare the Defence Forces to fight fires, build a recovery plan, help with insurance and have a preventative fire burn-off program every season.*"

Tommy thought for a while. I could hear his mind ticking over.

"OK. Give me a brief. So, a brief for the pre-selectors and one for the big electorate out there."

Rachael Overton tapped again and sent me an email officially requesting the brief. It pinged in my in-box immediately.

The two funeral directors were obviously disappointed and their lap-tops started tapping again.

"OK. What about Moslems? You know, the illegal arrivals." Tammy said. She had been so quiet her question now sounded like a shot from a church steeple.

I looked at her but I started talking to Tommy which I realised was a mistake, a big mistake. "You want to lose your future colleagues their seats? Some of their electorates are twenty percent Islamic." I said.

"And the Chinese?" Tammy said. It was more a statement than a question.

"Same thing. Electorates like Chisholm have about..."

"Thirty percent Chinese speaking." Helen said.

"How many?" Rachael Overton said and pursed her lips as if imagining twenty five thousand Chinese in a shopping mall, before she typed it in.

They all seemed pleased with that. That was when there was a knock on the door and one of the young security guards came in and whispered in Brother Underwood's exposed ears. Underwood showed no emotion but he nodded at Lieutenant Squeaky who nodded at Tommy as he stood up.

"They're back again." Lieutenant Squeaky said, "I'll secure gate four and hangar three. The CCTV is set to edit mode and we've got interdiction in place." He didn't wait to be excused, just moved like a young leopard seal into action. By the time he reached the door Underwood was in his wake, the two way radios already squawking. It was red alarm but it was hard to tell what enemy was at the gate.

"Well. That went well," I said.

"We'll wait until they get back." Tommy said and lapsed into silence which was unusual for him.

Rachael Overton indicated tea anyone but there were no takers. She shrugged and took a phone call, listened and tried to pass the phone to Tommy. "It's Dwayne from the Dwayne Dwyer Dance Duo. They want to hire our facilities in town."

Tommy shook his head. "You decide."

We waited while Mrs. Overton negotiated with Dwayne from the Dwayne Dwyer Dance Duo and sealed the deal with a promise that *Coming Now* would do the catering, sandwiches and party pies would do the trick and did they know that they'll need insurance cover if it's a paying event?

We listened for a while to the tapping of Tammy's fingernails on the table then she looked at her Piaget watch with its wheels and cogs and stood up.

"I'm going to get some fresh air." She said and clicked clacked her way to the door.

"I'll join you," I said and followed her down the corridor past the corrals, most of which were now empty. A small number of young acolytes in T-shirts which said COMING NOW—ARE YOU READY? were crowded round laptops, manipulating a camera obviously installed in a drone.

"Yes. Get a shot of the bus registration. Make sure you get the chicken." An older teenager with a touch of colour in his short cut hair said.

A younger one said, "Roger" and moved the cursor.

Outside, I caught up with Tammy Rayfinger who had a cigarette in her mouth. She blew a professional cloud over her shoulder.

"Don't ask." She said. It wasn't friendly.

"I won't ask." I said and then I understood what the young devotees had been working on inside.

Across the forecourt the front gate had been closed and a group of protesters were milling outside. Most were young and you could have sold a thousand brightly coloured socks and bumfreezer jackets on the spot. They had placards which said GAYS ARE PROUD and WHAT CHURCH HATES? and COMING NOW-IF ONLY. Protesters, walking back and forth in a crouch, were busy chalking rainbow colours on the black tarmac while others took photographs with their smart phones. There were about twenty of them. Two mini buses were parked nearby but a small drone hovered over them. It was all pretty orderly or at least it was until Lieutenant Squeaky (Reserves) mounted the counterattack. He was directing something behind him, feet wide apart like Napoleon at Austerlitz.

From one of the hangars another drone appeared and started to buzz the protesters who were forced to retreat to safety behind the mini-buses. This was followed up by a group of *Coming Now* acolytes in the T-shirts. They had their own placards which looked a little more professionally done as if prepared for the placard contest. The Battle of Bagdad had begun.

The *Coming Now* group outnumbered the protestors but they

were leaving nothing to chance. Lieutenant Squeaky (Reserves) was determined that the Battle of Bagdad was his to win. He stood for a moment and was now Napoleon crossing the Alps and pointing at the protestors and holding the pose longer than Napoleon ever did. His troops began a long slow chant which sounded like *a sin is a sin, where you bin?* Two of them were using small video cameras to capture the events, presumably for later editing.

"They come here every Gay Pride Day." Tammy exhaled another cloud of smoke. She was non-committal as if the protesters were delivering the morning mail.

"Thanks for letting me know." I said to no-one in particular as the chanting got louder. She ignored me then looked at that watch again. Every time we met she was wearing a different watch, all of them were a *if you have to ask the price you can't afford it, Big Ben size face included.*

The chanting from both sides rose until finally they let the Chicken Man out of one of the vans. The Chicken Man was a regular feature of a particular gay pride group. Like a football mascot, the ungainly yellow big bird cautiously descended from the mini-bus and raised his hands.

That was the moment when a giant goose entered the fray. Lieutenant Squeaky lifted his right arm and made a forward motion and someone in a white goose outfit trundled towards the gate and waved its wings at Chicken Man who advanced to the locked gate which was then slung open by the *Coming Now* acolytes, and The Goose attacked the Chicken Man. The two locked each other in a variety of clumsy super holds. It was Half Nelson to Half Nelson to the Stretch Plum. The Bite the Dragon, the Crucifix Arm-bar, the Chicken-wing and the Chinese Torture Grip and finally The Goose had the Chicken Man in a version of the Camel Clutch surrender hold. The Chicken tapped the tarmac because he didn't have God on his side and hadn't watched Mario Milano, Killer Karl Kox and Abdullah the Butcher on remastered World Championship Wrestling videotapes with his grandfather like I had. The *Coming Now* acolytes were ecstatic and patted The Goose on the back until he finally released the dishevelled Chicken man who retreated a little to recover and shake his feathers into place as his comrades checked him out for injuries.

"Who the hell is that?" I said

Tammy was intent on watching the finale so she didn't look at me. "It's Lucy Goosey." She said evenly as if the world knew that, somewhere in little old Bagdad, there was wrestling goose called Lucy.

"Be first story on the news tonight." I said.

She turned to me. "Nope, it'll be pinging on social media right this very moment. Mockery begets mockery."

"Mockery gets you on the front page of the *Mercury*, that's what it does. You know, this can't go on. Why hire us if you pull stunts like this?"

She stared at me, unblinking in the now bright sunlight. "I know you. You need the money, real bad honey and you're stubborn so you'll work harder to make it all happen. Simple as that. We'll take that risk."

"You'll risk everything, like Tommy making it to Canberra."

She twisted her thin neck and shrugged her shoulders. This was a woman who dressed simply, like a pastor's wife but who wore enough expensive watches and luxury jewellery to exhaust a horse. Risk came naturally and hidden agendas were just below the surface.

Lucy Goosey retreated inside the compound gates and the final stage of the Battle of Bagdad was about to commence as Lieutenant Squeaky raised his arm and another drone emerged from the hanger across the way and hovered above the besieged protestors like a sheep dog rounding up its sheep. As it hovered, a container on a thin line was lowered towards them. The container was eagerly snatched by the protestors who gathered round and tried to detach it. They obviously succeeded because there was a joint cry from the protestors and the acolytes. But the acolytes had the first and last laugh.

"What's that?" I said.

Tammy turned and pursed her lips. She held the remains of her cigarette in a pose like a 1950's movie star, elbow cradled in one hand and the cigarette in the air.

"Cold coffee." She said.

Before the battle was over she turned and invited me back inside. I noticed Lieutenant Squeaky was still directing the campaign but it was winding down. There were no prisoners taken, no wounded or killed, only hurt pride and confusion, a chance to test new weapons and be on the evening news, which was a problem for all of us.

Brother Underwood walked towards us. His gait was that rolling boot driven swagger that told you he meant business.

"Done." he said to Tammy and ignored me as we all walked back inside.

Not long after, Lieutenant Squeaky, the victor of the Battle of Bagdad joined us. Helen was explaining that any polling that showed only two percentage points difference between the Political Parties wasn't to be trusted.

I could see that the victorious Lieutenant Squeaky was highly agitated, if sucking on your teeth is proof of that.

"You've got something on your mind?" I said directly to him.

He shifted in his seat, and thought for a moment. Strangely, the others deferred to him and waited.

"Let me be very blunt." he said.

"Blunt away." I said.

"Let me say this. It's all about love." He paused to let that sink in.

Say that again Squeaky? Purse your mouth grimly and let your loving shine through.

"And fear and loathing?" Helen asked.

He looked at her as if she was invisible.

"We give them love...and protection."

Helen nodded. "Protection from whom?"

Lieutenant Squeaky sighed and shook his head slowly like your worst nightmare insurance agent when he tells you you're not covered because the flood was an Act of God.

"From the Devil out there and inside us. From the pornographers, child abusers, from thieves and violent people, from athiests and false religions and those that undermine family life. Our people have built a good life for themselves and have honoured their families. And when you look closer and know us better you'll see that, every one of them, they have one thing in common. They want our guidance and protection. And it's our duty to provide it in any way we can. And," He eyeballed me and pointed a thin finger directly at me, "And we have 72,000 people who say amen to that. Seventy two thousand. So Mr. Kennedy, tell us why we ought to change?"

The room was still. Pastor Tommy shrugged in a subtle way. It was a way of telling us that he agreed with the creed that Squeaky had picked up in some Bible College stuck out in the boondocks. Predictable, but you knew that twenty four hours in a room with Lieutenant Squeaky would have left you battered and bruised and a full filing cabinet of prepared responses would fall on you and prove once and for all that Jehova is a vengeful God. I turned to Tommie. "You agree with him?"

Tommy cleared his throat and turned the palms of his big hands outwards. "I'm still listening to you. But what do the others think? Brother Underwood. You raised these issues first so let's run it up the flag and see how it flutters."

Brother Underwood resumed where he'd left off fifteen minutes ago. I missed the first few words because I was still working out how a man could talk and be so still. Not an arm or hand flick or head movement, just this well-muscled and rigid being from whom words emitted like a cartoon bubble. Brother Underwood could have guided a drone to wipe out a village and go home for a warm milk and a night of TV watching, all without blinking. The transatlantic accent helped the image along.

Brother Underwood was just warming up. *The world was waiting anxiously, just waiting believe me, for Pastor Tommy's views on the major issues of our time which was abortion, euthanasia, Moslems, sexual depravity and homosexual marriage and neat and tidy lawns and young people who just didn't want to work and wouldn't get a hair-cut or defend their nation and why only yesterday Mrs. Overton here had received fifteen emails about the sacrilege committed by those awful people at the Mona or Moma or whatever it was Festival in Hobart and it's not even happening till Winter.* Helen exchanged glances with Robert. *There are many tribes but this one isn't ours.* Then Underwood fixed his eyes on me.

"Yep. Musilims," He said. It sounded like Musilims. "Today, out there, we fought the devil and won. Now we've got to fight this enemy." He held up his smart phone and was about to turn it on before Mrs Overton said politely, "We saw it in September and again in November and December."

But Brother Underwood, poised with the phone, said he was certain we would really understand how bad those Musilims were if we'd only just look at what's on his iPhone and they practiced decapitation you know. I could show you right now what they do. In public. Decapitation. We need to fight fire with fire. Our own version of decapitation, that's what we need.

Underwood placed the phone flat on the table and resumed his stone like position as if nothing had happened.

I looked around the room and Helen and Robert were open mouthed and on the point of throwing in the towel. *We are amongst cannibals.* Even Mrs Overton seemed disconcerted as if one of the Electric Evangelicals had stuck his grubby fingers into a live power point.

I tapped the table. "I'll go back to our original point. You will not make Pastor Tommy the next Prime Minister if you won't go outside the Bible Bubble. The swinging voters out there in Voterland don't give a rat's ar...don't care a fig about your obsessions. So, you pay us well to show you the way. At least listen and open your minds."

"That's blasphemy." Brother Underwood said grimly. There was a lot of menace there, even his mouth looked like it could open suddenly and a wolf leap out. He was looking for a reaction from Pastor Tommy who, through it all, was staying neutral.

"What's blasphemy? Thinking outside the box?" I said.

Underwood turned his body to Tommy then to Tammy then back at me. "Calling it...the Bible Bubble. Be warned. One day there will be laws in this country which will outlaw such blasphemy." His eyes set me in his sights. "You want us to drop all our basic beliefs? Everything we stand for?" He said.

"I want you to do more than that. I want you to let me know before you organise stupid stunts like that one outside the gates a while ago. That, Brother Underwood, was a total disaster and if you don't believe me, watch tonight's TV news or check your iPhone. Even if you don't take our advice, just let us know first when you pull stunts like that." On Helen's phone, the pinging continued. She angled the phone so I could see out of the corner of my eye. The Battle of Bagdad was already news which was quickly followed by internet gossip and fake news about the Battle. Fortunately, most of the news didn't mention Tommy Rayfinger.

Police say they are unaware of the incident outside a religious community's headquarters in Bagdad. LGBTI activists have formally complained to Tasmania's Anti-Discrimination Commissioner about what they describe as an unprovoked attack on their members.

Lieutenant Squeaky ignore the pinging news items. He had another challenge to make. "And what advice would that have been?"

How about letting you sink your own Titanic and you can all pray together while you steal other people's life-boats. Or Lieutenant Squeaky, make your life worthwhile with some last minute rutting before she goes down. But we had a life-saving five hundred grand to keep the old conscience attacks away so I put on my good boy mask.

Helen and Robert were impassive but they had booked front row tickets so they waited. *Over to you Red Rover.*

I looked squarely at the funeral directors but Mrs Overton kept catching my eye as if someone was about to say *nice day for biblicals and happy families with picnic baskets are welcome.*

"Look it's going to be a nice week and we've drawn up a voter engagement plan, so I suggest we go to some little towns I know where you can step out of Clapperland into Voterland. Point is, are you game or are we wasting our time?"

There was silence in the room except for an anachronistic clock ticking somewhere, the pinging of Helen's mobile and a fly hitting the summer window panes.

"So," Helen said brightly.

I looked at her. We needed to get out in the fresh air.

"Primrose Sands or Sorell or Bothwell or Oatlands or Westbury or maybe even New Norfolk." I announced. "Like a *Coming Now* grand picnic. Great places to go where a real man can meet real people. Right Tommy?"

I looked at Tommy. He had the vacant face of a professional footballer too confused to listen to the coach. He didn't move and he said nothing to the funeral directors or Tammy. There had obviously been a phone call before we arrived.

Brother Underwood pursed his lips a little but that cropped head and gimlet eyes stared fixedly back at me. Rachael Overton relaxed bolt upright and folded her hands. You got the impression that World War Three could have broken out and she could tell you how many tanks each side had or how many sandwiches would be required for the troops. Lieutenant Squeaky rocked his head so slightly you could have missed it. His thin pale arms and fingers toyed with one of those click biros. Click, click. Nothing but clicking and Helen's pinging phone with more fake news about the Battle of Bagdad.

Mrs. Overton suddenly looked across the table at Helen and closed her laptop. It was a kindly matronly gesture. "So, my dear. Never try to stop a galloping horse." It broke the silence but nobody knew what the hell she was trying to say. Being an archivist had its benefits.

Helen got up and wiped the whiteboard with a handkerchief. She looked at me as if this day of quotes was going to end with Advertising Rule Number Five. *Only leave a record if your advice proves to be correct.*

TEN

The watchman watches in vain

We were sitting outside in a cafe in Salamanca Place. Helen, Robert and me. It was busy and the tourists were off the cruise ships and into the cafes and gift shops looking for woollen scarves in summer and Huon pine candlesticks. That part of town is a sandstone Georgian precinct set amongst plane trees and the lawns of Parliament House were already full of people just relaxing in the sun. Hobart was the last of the old whaling ports and there were ship chandlers and other active sea based businesses still in the old warehouses. Nowadays they are outnumbered by the cafes, ferry terminals and other beneficiaries of the gig economy.

"Why are we here? I asked them.

"Because we need a noisy café," Robert said waving his hands to indicate that the pumping loud muzak was an attraction.

"Well I don't. Can we pick another one? How about Maldinis?" Maldinis was an Italian place down the street that had great sea food pastas like spaghetti a la vongole. It also had table service and soft music that recognised there are some people in the world aged over thirty.

"I think when we finish telling you something you'll appreciate the loud music." Helen said. A waiter appeared who had the capacity to lean like the Tower of Pisa without falling over. It was a prodigious feat.

"What can I do you for? Are you eating?"

"No, not at this very moment," Robert said. I wasn't sure that he meant it as a joke, because he was highly anxious, turning his head instinctively.

The waiter leaned forward further than the Tower of Pisa and tried to still his disdain. "Yeeees?" He said.

Robert said, "Yes, yes. Coffees all round, thank you."

The waiter resumed the vertical position. "Which type of coffee sir? Or let's take pot-luck shall we?"

Robert was already opening his laptop. He waved vaguely in the waiter's direction. "Yes, yes. You choose."

I smiled and indicated to the waiter that I had eccentric friends. "Three lattes thanks."

The waiter almost crouched like a tennis player, clenched his fist and punched the air in a short sharp burst. "Gotcha!" and disappeared in a couple of bounds.

"OK. What's so urgent that we have to leave the office and drink coffee in a musical jungle?" I said.

Robert pushed his laptop towards me.

"What's this mean?" I asked. The screen was full of programing gobbledygook.

"Just a moment, "Robert said and pulled out his mobile phone, held it to his face then punched in a PIN and followed it with a fingerscan.

He saw me watching. "Three factor authentication, face and finger biometrics and a PIN." He explained.

"Yes. What does it mean?"

"Well, a biometric is..."

"I know what a biometric is, Robert. Cut to the chase. Why are we here?"

Robert nodded. "Helen and I have been busy. The long and the short of it is, we have been hacked."

"Big time hacked." Helen said. I looked at her. She shrugged like she was also surprised. "We have been spied on. Our internal WAN has been compromised, our office has been bugged. With one of these beauties." She handed me a tiny device that was about the size of two thumbnails.

"Sophisticated?"

Robert took it from me and rolled it into a snow white handkerchief. Somehow I always knew that any handkerchief of Roberts would be snow white. Then he handed it back "This device is very sophisticated. I've never seen one before but it's not only a microphone; it's also a camera. Military grade." He said.

Helen waited while the waiter landed the coffees safely from roof high. "Three wonderful lattes." He announced and loped away again.

"Just be careful when we go back. We left the other bugs in place so our spies are not going to cotton on. I'll give this little baby to your mate Dinny Dinham. Get his take on it" She said.

"Bloody great! Bugged in our own office. The bastards! Who?" It was a silly question.

Robert played with his phone again and the coding on my screen turned into real letters and numbers.

"What does this mean?"

"It means that someone has placed a Trojan Horse into our network. They've tried to cover their tracks, you know, using a DNS name that is hiding the IP address of the RAT."

"What's that?"

"Never mind. This has been done by someone who isn't as smart as they think they are. We know exactly who it is because we have back engineered the program and we have full administrator access to their network. So, my very strong suggestion is we leave it all in place and monitor those bastards all the way," Helen said. "We will now have a living breathing entrée to the world of *Coming Now*. Robert is still digging into their financials, because we want those too."

"That would be illegal, wouldn't it?" I asked.

Helen smiled "Legal takes a little longer."

"The coffee's actually very good." Robert said. "I should tell you something else. I was followed by a drone this morning when I left my flat."

I was about to say, *you're being paranoid, this is Tasmania* but we were entering the weird wonderful world of *Coming Now* and anything was possible, even miracles.

"I bloody told you so." Dinny Denham said, "You on a secure phone?"

"Yes", I said. "Robert gave me a special device."

Dinny sighed. "He's a strange one that Pommie Bob. Is he a spook or something? He seems to know a lot about all this security stuff."

"Don't even ask."

"Are you in an animal house?"

"I am sitting like a vagabond in the Mall and there are more school kids here than on a papal visit. Now, tell me about that bug."

"Well, it's very sophisticated. My guys say they've never come across its type before. Something that small that's both a camera and a microphone and voice activated with a battery. Very smart stuff."

I noticed a group of teenagers amongst the ones who hang out and pretend they are of smoking age which provides the cops with something to do in peaceful, daytime, down town Hobart. Maybe, the police are there to protect the young preachers who have a permanent position at one end. It's a desultory place sheltered by the curving plastic roof and some cut-price attempts by the architects to make a better world. There's a lone Council approved busker, cheaper teenage based clothing shops and phone shops dedicated to service and expensive mobile plans. What drew my attention was a young woman who I swore I'd seen working on the computer screens at the *Coming Now* compound.

"You still there?" Dinny said.

"I'll call you back. Thanks mate."

"You've got two more favours and then we're square, right?"

"Gotcha."

The young blonde haired woman was standing with a group of friends watching the preacher.

"Hi," I said.

There was a moment of hesitation then she brightened.

"Oh, sorry. You're the man who came to see Pastor Rayfinger the other day, with the red haired lady."

She was wearing clothes that picked her out as a McDonald's or some burger chain employee. Her badge said Jacinta.

"You're off to work?"

"No, I've just finished. I do a few hours at McDonald's in town here."

She was so open and bright-eyed. You had to give it to *Coming Now*. They trained kids well and the work ethic was obvious or maybe they just had good families that loved them.

"You must be a making a few bob. Two jobs."

She seemed to be confused. "A few bob?"

"Yes, wages."

She laughed. "Oh no, I don't get a wage at *Coming Now*. And the McDonald's money helps me pay my tithes."

I took a stab in the dark. "Helen told me that some of you do cat videos."

She looked surprised. "Is Helen the soldier lady? She's really nice."

"I think so too."

She gave me a broad pink faced smile. "Are you and the soldier lady...like, together?"

"Like, together," I said.

"That's really nice." A glowing reference I filed for later.

The young preacher on the soap box was starting to get some stick from the skate-board fraternity and older school kids. The young woman watched it with silent disapproval.

"I'm fascinated," I said, "Why do you make cat videos and sport stories?"

She hesitated then explained. Looking at her I could tell she was incapable of telling an untruth or even being cagey. "Well. We want people to share and be loved. When they like the videos we get their details and we help them be part of a group where everyone cares about the same thing. Like a big happy family. You know, a lot of people on the internet are lonely and it's nice for them to know there are people out there who care about the same things as they do. You know we also have dog videos and videos about free animals like wombats and koalas and kangaroos."

"And what do you do with all their details, you know their email addresses and so on?"

She rubbed her snub nose which highlighted her purple painted fingernails, "Oh, that gets sent on to the Big Friend. That's what we call it. You know. It's a big computer somewhere that helps us tell people about the Lord Jesus."

"Big Friend." I said. "Yep. Sounds really friendly."

ELEVEN

Whiter than snow

"Oh, God! That is so, so good! Look at us! Just look at us together! Aaargh! Argh! Yes, yes! C'mon, c'mon! C'mon!" A woman's voice then a man's deep voice that I could recognise said, "Yes. You are mine! Look at us! Just look at us!"

There was no doubt what was going on in the other office. It was an opera invented a long time ago but it took me aback when I came in and Donna was barely able to look at me. Her flushed face behind the reception desk told me that her operas were private if they happened at all before her marriage. Then I heard laughter from the other office. It was Helen and Robert but the entertainment ploughed on regardless, with even more moaning and a lot of words that you wouldn't hear in a Country Women's Association conference.

"Donna. What the hell is that?"

"It's Mr. Malahide and Mrs. Troy." She could barely look at me as the laughter and love-making broke through the sound barriers of the glass door of the office that Helen and Robert shared with enough computers and equipment to service the Pentagon. For a moment I was flushed and bewildered but even before Donna clarified the situation I had a feeling that we were already in a world of black comedy.

Donna still avoided my eyes. It was unsettling to know that somewhere down in the Huon Valley there were young people like Donna who still used words like fiancé and marriage and house deposit and Sunday services and saving ourselves for later.

"It's not Mr. Malahide and Mrs. Troy," she said by way of explanation and looked away again.

I knocked on the door and went in. Robert and Helen were sitting side by side watching a screen. Helen was still shaking her head in disbelief as the sex built to a crescendo of moaning and grunting.

They both turned as I entered.

They were flushed and still laughing.

"Just bloody look at this!" Helen said. "Guess who?"

I didn't need to guess. The couple on the screen were still making the beast in the field, their faces both looking directly at the screen. The Reverend Pastor Tommy Rayfinger was already bringing an evangelical meaning to the laying on of hands. I looked more closely. They were deliberately looking at the camera and when the woman tossed her head away, the Pastor put his big hands under her chin and pointed her towards the camera again. That made it easier to figure that she was not Tammy Rayfinger unless Tammy was a blonde and a well-known public figure.

Finally they finished with some highly athletic thrusts from Pastor Tommy.

"I didn't realise that Pastor Tommy was so gifted an athlete." Helen said and screen shot the last frame. "Guess who the lady is?"

"I know who the lady is." I said.

Robert was still grinning. "She's also in the Party. Awfully nice way to win over the pre-selectors but a trifle fatiguing if...how many are there in Lyons?"

"About thirty."

"Does he need any help?" Robert laughed and swung his chair

around. I liked that chair. It wasn't the usual cloth and swivel standard chair but some nineteenth century dark oak that he'd brought out from the UK. *Protection from the mould and damp* he said which just about summed up his relationship with his home country.

I sat down but the screen shot of Pastor Tommy and his Solomon's bride was disconcerting. I reached over and delicately turned it around.

"So, tell me why and how?"

Helen gave me one of those saintly glances that contained both innocence and barrack room salaciousness.

"Because they were excited with each other and the man becomes erect and..."

"Stop mucking around. How the hell did we manage to get this grotesque invasion of privacy?"

"Doesn't look that grotesque to me."

"No. You know what I mean. This is an invasion of privacy...big time invasion. And I thought we agreed that we would be careful given that our office is bugged."

Robert sighed and started to take me through the background. "Well, we were working on all the content for the TV and social media advertising. We wanted live video of Pastor Rayfinger."

"Well you certainly got that."

He grimaced, "Well they sent all this across. You know kids playing, Pastor Rayfinger out in the community shaking hands, social events, that type of thing. Well, we'd done most of the editing and it was all in the can and then this came across. I don't think they realised that it was all networked."

Helen laughed. "I reckon the old Pastor Tommy thought it was a stand-alone camera and as sure as hell he wasn't gonna ask for advice from people like Lieutenant Squeaky...or Tammy Rayfinger."

Robert suddenly became very serious, perhaps bewildered.

He switched off the laptop and swivelled his chair towards me. His brow furrowed. "Well, old man. In terms of technology, yes, he's probably a little challenged but it's not encrypted, it's unprotected. How could they possibly be so careless as to allow that little episode into their network?"

"Blood drains from the head when..." Helen started.

Robert looked pained. "A propos bugs. We've temporally disabled them and insulated the office with a virtual surround. I know you said to keep those planted cameras going, but it's impossible to do that all time. The two of us just can't work in that environment. And, if I remember correctly, you asked us explicitly to back channel the *Coming Now* network to investigate them comprehensively." He peered at me across his tiny reading glasses. "Comprehensively. But...if you wish us to delete this little pantomime, I'm happy to do it."

Helen sat bolt upright. The smile lines on either side of her mouth became tighter. "No bloody way. This little performance of Pastor Tommy and his mate stays. We'll cache it. These bastards have been invading *our* privacy, big time. It stands to reason. Last weekend, you gave them honest, unbiased professional advice and they absolutely refused to take it. They're entitled to do that. But they then bug our office. They're not entitled to do that." She waved a hand to stop me interrupting. "Absolutely not entitled. I understand that we need the money. That we have to stay working for them, well, long enough, but they freak me out and you know what, I think they're bloody capable of anything."

I looked around their technical den. Computers and servers everywhere. Blinking modems and routers. Charts on the wall. But, there was a whiteboard with flow charts and arrows pointing to slogans, problem issues, the data we had on voters, all part of the *Coming Now* project. I was always amazed that these two had a battery of computers and designer programs at their fingertips but whenever they wanted to exchange real ideas they retreated to a 20th century whiteboard. There was no other sign of anything personal except Robert's oak chair. Compared with that, my own office was almost a retreat and a second home with objects and things I'd picked up and paid too much for. Helen described my office as the Old Curiosity Shop and me as a pack rat, which was pretty accurate. *And you don't like change either*, she'd say, which was a bit rich coming from someone who refused to sleep overnight at my place, ever.

"You finished?" I said.

She stood up. She was wearing khaki green drill pants like an army uniform. Her Blundstone boots and black T-shirt topped off that impression. She turned on a tight circle like a relaxed ballerina. Prowling in that crowded office was impossible. Then she pointed at Robert. "Yes, there is another thing. Tell him what you think, Robert."

Robert nodded his head sideways, trying to avoid the question. He tweaked his cuff links and stroked his MCC tie, for it *was* an MCC tie.

"It's probably nothing," he said almost aimlessly.

"What's nothing?" I said.

He stroked his chin. "Well, I believe a drone followed me home last night."

I got up so Helen and I were almost face to face. She put her hands firmly on her hips and waited. Her arms had a soft down that emphasised the fact that she never wore any ornaments or perfume, nothing but a cheap watch with a plastic band.

"Ok." I said, "I want you to track every movement *Coming Now* makes. Every time they so much as fart or pray, I want them tracked. Turn on those bugs again and watch what you say, any time, but make it look like we are still unaware of them. I want new phones that are not connected to our network and we only communicate on them through encrypted messaging. Oh, and move the money manually into a separate bank account. One that's not online. Leave enough in the online account to allay their suspicions, you know, for salaries and expenses. This afternoon I'll ring Pastor Tommy and ask for another $100 grand which means we need to continue the work for them. But don't bust a gut, just good professional work. No arguments, give into them if they have different views. Oh, and when we want to talk privately, we meet in a secure place."

Helen was texting on her mobile phone. She looked up at me and smiled. "Don't worry. It's WhatsApp. Encrypted."

"And one last thing you two. Robert can start. I want all the financial and tax records of *Coming Now*. All their business plans, their investment portfolio, like exactly where are they getting their money from? And, their payroll and wages. Who is on their payroll? How many are volunteers who do not get paid. But, discretion. Got it?"

When I went to lunch, Donna was still blushing and avoiding my eyes with grim determination.

"Donna, what's up?"

She still avoided my eyes.

"Mr. Kennedy, I don't think it's right. Not right at all," She was almost breathless then she added. "Everyone laughing in there. It's spying on Pastor and Mrs. Rayfinger. How would Mrs Rayfinger feel?"

"What do you mean? How would she feel?"

"Mr. Kennedy. You know what I mean. Her being on film."

"Mrs. Rayfinger on film? That wasn't Mrs..." Then I paused.

She looked up, her face red, almost in tears but she was determined to have her say. "Yes, it would be awful to be on film and people laughing. It's spying you know. What would Mrs. Rayfinger think if she knew she was on film...doing that?"

"Donna, I agree with you. Mrs. Rayfinger would be very upset by that spying. We all hate spying" I said and hurried to lunch with my old lawyer.

"Sign it." Erica Bendall pushed the one page document across the table.

"Tell me why."

"Because, for the life of me, I do not know why they paid you five hundred thousand to make my client Prime Minister. You're a grumpy bugger but a smooth talker."

I peered across the top of my reading glasses at thin, acerbic, smart-as-a-fox Erica and tried to read her.

"Erica, I thought I was your client."

Erica tapped the document with her long blue finger nails. Who at the age of fifty had blue finger nails?

"You *were* my client but we closed the file when you complained and called us off. I was then free to take up the *Coming Soon* offer. A girl has to eat."

I looked around the restaurant. There was nobody I knew there and the salmon fritters we had both ordered were doing a tour of duty over the top of my shoulder. Erica sipped her water and shrugged her striped power suit which sat on her shoulders like a Romanian aristocrat.

"Any dinner parties at Sandy Bay lately?" She said archly. I ignored her.

"Did you draft this?" I said.

"I wrote under the client's instructions." She reached across and took a fritter off my plate which nicely summed up our relationship.

"Who gave the instructions?"

She snorted and cut her fritter into neat manageable proportions like a chess player positioning the pieces.

"I can't tell you that."

"You can't tell. I can't sign."

"Keep your voice down and are you going to eat your salad?"

I looked at the contract again. It was one page, in fact, one paragraph after you left room for the title and the signatures.

Patrick Kennedy and Associates Pty Ltd, hereinafter called the service supplier, agrees to provide Coming Now Incorporated with services to the service supplier's best endeavour. Those services include:

    a) *planning to assist Pastor Tommy Sanders Rayfinger to win pre-selection as the Liberal Party of Australia's candidate for the Federal Electorate of Lyons;*

    b) *planning to assist Pastor Tommy Sanders Rayfinger to win selection as the Federal Member for the seat of Lyons; and*

    c) *providing certain other services as agreed mutually between the parties.*

For the above services, Coming Now Incorporated has paid Patrick Kennedy and Associates Pty Ltd the amount of $500,000 dollars. Further remuneration may be negotiated mutually by both parties.

The contract said nothing about failure to deliver on our part, mediation procedures or penalty clauses or any of the other caveats that made lawyers rich and clients worried. At first glance it looked like an insurance policy, but for whom?

Erica waved at one of her mates across the room. Outside, there was a volunteer group fixing the rigging of the replica eighteenth century brig berthed in front of us. One of the crew was already crawling out on the mainsail, taking his time because he was old enough to be there when the French were beaten to the claiming of Tasmania. *No need to hurry. The French have gone.*

"Must have a big mouth." Erica said.

"Who?"

"They must have a big mouth to eat a burger like that."

At the next table three young suits were about to tuck into twenty five dollar burgers and a bottle of red.

I read the contract again.

"You didn't write this," I said. "It's too short and vague amongst other things."

"Have you looked at the initials on the cc address?"

"RRO? Who the hell is that?"

She laid down her knife and starting forking the pieces into her mouth, good clean technique.

"You don't know? That's because you are an impatient, condescending misogynist who takes no notice of women in the room." She said.

"As bad as that?" Then it struck me. "RRO. Mrs. Rachael Overton. She gave the instructions?"

"They tell me you've got yourself a little soldier girl?" Erica said a propos nothing. "You never seemed the type to like girls in uniforms."

"I admire nurses and cops and fireys in uniform because they do good things." I said.

"Hmm."

"So just to confirm. You didn't draft this?"

Erica looked blithely at me. This was Erica Bendall, blood hound who would chase convicts and moneyed people with equal fervour. "I'm not at liberty to confirm or deny this. Nor can I advise you. Obviously, you will sign it, won't you?"

"Where do I sign?" I said and took the fountain pen she already had poised in the air.

TWELVE

A wheel in the middle of a wheel

The Liberal Party of Australia is a strange beast, almost like the mythical creature that changed its nature before your very eyes. It grew out of an elitist bankers' party that regarded politicians as their hired servants. That is until Bob Menzies, a small town lawyer from Jeparit changed its name and recruited all the forgotten little people as he called them, shopkeepers, school teachers, farmers, bank clerks, returned soldiers and anyone else who prized sturdy independence provided the government looked after them and then left them alone.

Today, the Big End of Town still runs the show again except mining companies, media magnates and hedge fund bosses occupy centre stage again.

I wasn't interested in the Big End of Town that week. I needed to know whether or not the pre-selectors in Lyons were going to accept Pastor Tommy Rayfinger as their chosen candidate. A lot were disciples of the power brokers in the Party but a lot were genuine rusted on Libs who made their own decisions.

George Rathbone was one of the few potential pre-selectors I could talk to openly even if I had to put up with his leg pulling about my Bolshevik tendencies. So, on a day that blew rain and thunder like the Day of Judgement I headed east towards George's farm. George habitually called it a property which better described the strange combination of Georgian sandstone mansion with a collection of untidy outbuildings and machinery sheds that surrounded the rear of the homestead like the last days of Mad Max. It was a prosperous sheep and cattle farm with a sizable vineyard and plenty of well managed dams and irrigation systems that stalked the paddocks like praying mantises on heat. But, unlike praying mantises, George never disposed of anything; machinery, old wool presses, clapped out tractors that knew Henry Lawson, it was all there like a museum of the agricultural mind.

"Good to see that the museum's still open." I said pointing at the sheds. It had stopped raining but the grey and blue kaleidoscopic sky above the green gentling rolling hills said it wouldn't last.

George's handshake was welcoming but dangerous.

"Mock away, bum polisher. One day."

"Oh, Massey-Fergusons without an engine. Big call for them."

"We don't make anything in Australia anymore. Thanks to your lefty mates." He said and tipped his sweat stained Akubra. He wore it like a real Aussie unlike the fake Aussies who campaign in blue checked shirts, RM Williams boots and a clean Akubra perched symmetrically like a pigmy possum on their heads. George's moleskins and checked shirt always looked like they'd been freshly washed but still came out looking a thousand years old.

"Grapes coming along nicely?" I said to change the subject.

"Don't know. James does all that. But, I made him set up his own irrigation system. And you know what he did? You know what he did when he couldn't get the water he needed? He went bloody organic!" We both chortled about that until George reckoned we needed a cuppa.

We walked along the drive towards the veranda where I knew we didn't need to take our boots off. Although George was a lot older than me I noticed his farmers walk had become more exaggerated with his bow legs ambling along and his bum stuck out like he'd wet his pants. It was the walk of people who actually dug and lifted and pushed things for a living.

We sat on the sandstone flagged veranda in cane chairs and peeked at the distant hills through passionfruit vines that were climbing the cast iron columns. I knew the tea would arrive soon, unordered because George's wife Meredith would have seen us, allowed a few minutes for preliminary bickering and then prepared the afternoon tea in a tea set that had survived a couple of centuries.

"Meant to thank you for what you did for the Church." He said.

"Could have sent an email, they're free."

"Don't touch them" He said. "I read."

"Dickens isn't reading. It's a life sentence." I said.

"Better characters. You know Fagan came to Tasmania? He wasn't hanged, like in the book." George was the only person I knew who could properly subjugate the verb to hang.

"Your life is wasted." I said.

"So what's the option?? I reckon it's better than kissing the bums of every wealthy buffoon in town, like some." He peered at me as if he were wearing spectacles. "Anyway, thanks for the Church thing. That little campaign means a lot. It's the community's cemetery and a lot of our people built that with their own hands."

"With convict hands."

"Someone had to give the orders. Funny thing, the Labor MP, what was her name?"

"Jenna Butler"

"Yes. Butler. She got it. She understood that no bloody bishop's going to sell off our church. What that does to the community, she understood it."

"Glad to hear that the Bolsheviks get it." I said. We had done a freeby for a few local communities who were fighting back when the new Bishop was trying to sell off a swathe of churches and other property round the state.

Tea arrived at precisely the time that George and I had agreed on something. Meredith was a tall angular but elegant middle aged woman who always had her prematurely hair cut to a no-nonsense style to match the belted skirt and Kashmir pullovers that allowed white collars to stand higher than normal.

"Lovely to see you again Patrick. George misses you."

"No I don't."

She patted him absently on the shoulder while she smiled at me. "Yes you do. It's because I won't argue with him. I think the Rathbones were sent out here because they were prone to argument." She said it as if *prone to argument* could mean anything from losing the family fortune on cards to shooting someone in a duel. Tasmania had a long history of second and third sons being granted land because they missed out when the eldest son inherited the lot. So the dispossessed then dispossessed the original owners who faded into history and George and I could safely drink tea and gaze at the nineteenth century oaks that lined the driveway.

"Leave you to it." She said and went off to do what you do without servants in a home that once had a host of assigned servants, mainly of the convict type.

George took the tea and poured it. The tea set was a delicate flower pattern which made George's cracked knuckled hands with their ingrained grease look like monsters from outer space.

"I hear you're interested in finding out whether that Reverend evangelical is going to get pre-selection or not. Purely academic interest I guess."

"Purely academic." I said.

"He'll probably get up because the Christians will vote for him."

"George. You're a Christian."

"Not that type of Christian."

"Christians got the numbers?" I said.

"Don't know. Milk?"

"Never touch it. I've visited dairies. You know that."

"I forgot. Yes. You know, the Reverend Rayfinger rang last week."

I sipped the tea. It had rained all the way as I drove through the parched farmlands. Even the thousands of acres that had been despoiled by the pressure of the sheep flocks would be growing a thin film of green around the few lonely dead trees. Trees gone the way of the original forests and bushland, burnt by the aboriginals for hunting purposes then finally cleared for the sheep that made fortunes for the eventual winners.

"What's he like?"

George peered at me, not believing me. "He's got the gift of the gab. Done his homework about me. But he's not fair dinkum. That's all I can say. When he was talking to me on the phone, it was like he was talking from a script that someone else had written for him. Anyway. I'm not voting for him."

"Many like you?"

"Nope. I do my own thing. He's got money though and he can pull all the Christians so he'll get up."

"Can he win Lyons at the next election?"

"No, the next. We're not going to have a candidate this time because of the problem," He said referring to the perennial problem that every political party faces when their candidates do something stupid or unacceptable. "So he's going to have to wait."

There was a tractor towing a light harrow to enable early autumn sowing. You had to hand it to George. He'd read every book ever written about caring for the land and there were little copses here and there as windbreaks, and dams with shrubs and reeds, planted to aerate the water and hold the soil nearby. He had a few privileges on the way like his inheritance and boarding at Hutchins private school, if that was a privilege, but he did what he was born to do and he did it well.

"Do you remember the first time we met?" George said and poured himself another cup, blowing on the surface.

"Yeah. You bloody knocked my block off." We had a good laugh about that although George had mentioned it one or two times before. We were both playing in the TFL and George was a star with the Sandy Bay Club which recruited a lot of the private school kids and then toughened up the team with loggers, small farmers and fishermen from down the Channel. The club went broke later because the business men who ran it forgot that a business actually needed customers to turn up.

I said. "But you apologised. I still think that was amazing. An apology! Private schools do their job properly."

"Met your old man once, at the football. Hated being called Paddy." George said.

"Well, I hate being called Patrick so there we are." I said, avoiding genealogy.

"I tell you. That Reverend Rayfinger was a beauty back in the days when he was a real person. Best full back I ever saw. You know, St. Kilda recruited him when he was only sixteen. Sixteen! And he gave it all up to go round flogging bibles, and making a good living at it, too. Nope. I'm not voting for him and I'll be sitting on that pre-selection panel to have my say."

We could hear the tractor's motor as it took advantage of the newly wet soil. A utility headed up the hill and two men got out and walked around one of the biggest dead trees then started a chainsaw. The banshee sound revved and whined then ran on neutral while the other man inserted chocks. Then the process was repeated until there was a loud sharp crack and the tree leaned in slow motion before cracking and thumping on the ground.

"He'll be preselected though. He's got the money so we don't have find the campaign dollars from the Party, he's got all those bloody volunteers and he's got that contact list. You know the ones they use for Facebook. So, he's a certainty to be pre-selected."

That day it was Tommy Rayfinger the philanthropic businessman who together with his lovely wife Tammy was about to make a donation that would change ordinary people's lives. First, we needed a forum where all the Good and True would be gathered and we had that by making a little cash donation to a number of charities that wanted to pressure the State and Federal Governments about Tasmania's housing crisis. Tasmania was the flavour of the month but that helped investor and AirBnB money drive up rents and house prices. *Something must be done and we did it.*

Our one condition, tactfully put with no fingerprints, was that the forum should be held in Bridgewater which was one of the oldest housing commission welfare suburbs which boasted great views down to the Derwent River and the surrounding hills but threw in the occasional neighbour with good neighbour issues. In a political sense Bridgewater was not unique in Australia as Right Wing parties chipped away at Labor's traditional support by tough on immigration and anti-Chinese investment rhetoric and other variations based on racism and fear of change. *At least that Donald Trump does what he promises and American kids can get jobs, our kids can't get jobs.*

The roll call of the Good and True was long and guaranteed to get reasonable news coverage as the Good and the True would be rolling out their carefully thought out proposals, costed to the last dollar and backed by persuasive statistics. But we had an even better proposal that would be guaranteed to move this talk-fest straight onto tomorrow's front pages.

"All the print journalists here?" I asked. The camera people were all on the stage taking over-the-shoulder and establishing shots for the evening news. The speakers were already casually but self-consciously out the front with occasional forays to shake hands in the audience. TV journalists were checking their note pads just to ensure they got all the pollies and mayor's names right but they already had the main story which was THE TOMMY RAYFINGER CHALLENGE. Tommy had already done the TV stand-ups and the RAYFINGER CHALLENGE was already in the can and flying through virtual air all the way to the editing suites back in Hobart.

The recipient of this media largess was already at the front and for the short arsed in the audience it was impossible not to see him dwarfing the other pollies and mayors and charity CEOs that get drawn to these forums *because something must be done.*

It all got underway in that community hall in that unloved suburb that was created by unsocial planners.

"The issue is the number of homes that have been converted to short stay accommodation, turfing out long term tenants in favour of better paying short stay tourists. That's more than one thousand homes that are now unavailable to people seeking an actual home to rent."

"The State and Federal Governments must build more social housing, restore the old Housing Department building programs."

"First home owners grants only allow vendors to raise the selling price of their homes because they know that the young couple already have an extra twenty and thirty thousand from the Government burning a hole in their pocket."

"Did the State Government have an integrated housing plan, yes, a

plan to deal with Tasmania's growth that they knew was coming?"

"Did the University have a fully worked out Master Plan when they decided to encourage thousands of overseas students and decided to move the University campus into the city or did it just grow like Topsy?"

Then, after the Mayors, the sitting pollies called for more to be done, it's a disgrace and the Government will need to spend more and the Government needs to spend less and let the private sector deliver the solutions and open up more land and cut out the red tape that just stops development in its tracks. The speakers in their folding chairs at the front ran out of steam and Pastor, sorry, Tommy Rayfinger, philanthropic businessman rose to speak.

He did his leaning trick then his self-deprecating trick followed by a minute or two of how, day and night, Tommy and his wife Tammy and their kids thought about nothing but the homeless and what they as a family could do about it.

"I am just a businessman who when he sees a problem wants to do something about it." He said. He had the microphone in his hands and he wasn't going to give it up. He walked down the aisle and looked sincerely, pleadingly at these good people who gave their time and indeed their lives to helping the homeless. "Tammy and I and want to actually do something about it. It's only a little gesture but, by golly, we can make it snowball." He waited and looked around deliberately and slowly, avoiding the self-conscious rapid fire delivery of the other speakers who usually rattled along as if someone was always about to interrupt them.

Robert was filming Tommy as he walked down the aisle, following the giant turning head. He knew what was coming and, probably overcoming his tendency to put his finger down his throat, was getting close-ups.

"Yes." Said Tommy breathlessly, "We sat down as a family, Tammy and me and Ruthie and Debbie and we said let's make a Rayfinger

Challenge. And so today, we want to get the ball rolling. We are issuing a challenge to every home owner who has a house on short stay to let it out to long term tenants. Or build another house. Impossible, improbable? Never say never. Here's how we start."

Sensing that the chairman was about to cut him off, Tommy quickened the pace. "Today, we will issue the Rayfinger Challenge. We will provide immediately ten houses for long term tenants. Right here in Bridgewater. Then when another generous soul meets that we will build another ten. And we will do that within six months if we get council permission, because they will be houses designed to get approval easily. And after that, we will do another ten as long as other people match it each time. By the end of this year I reckon we will house over two hundred families." *Nearly all in the electorate of Lyons.*

There was a lot of applause from the locals and some of the mayors who had long ago cast off their egos. The other pollies put their hands together but Robert's microphone would not have detected a sound from those hands as they reluctantly touched, softly. *In the Melbourne Cup of Life, simple tactics and a good horse triumphs over the Good and the True. Advertising Rule Number Six.*

At the end of the meeting there was a lot of shuffling and connecting and lobbying and media hunting but the biggest pack was around Tommy who was mansplaining the Rayfinger Challenge.

Robert sent me an edited video on my phone.

It started with Tommy walking the aisle explaining the Rayfinger Challenge except this was another kind of challenge altogether.

As Tommy spoke, an obviously dubbed voice—actually Robert imitating the Charlton Heston of Tommy's voice—gave a different version.

"Yes. This is the Rayfinger Challenge. How does a man like me explain how I bought up houses cheap from tenants who couldn't meet their

mortgage payments? Then I let them stay and I double the rent. That's how the Rayfinger Challenge with Tammy and me and little Ruthie and Debbie manages to be a challenge, for us. But thanks to our friends at Paddy Kennedy and Co, we'll answer that challenge. That's right, we bought their scrubby little homes because we wanted to get them out of debt. Taurus excreta cerebrum vincit."

I went to a quiet corner and rang Robert back.

"Robert. Don't you go dirty on me!"

"Don't worry. It's my idea of a little joke. Just letting off steam. The real story's in the can. Looks good."

"Robert, that Catholic stuff? *Taurus excreta cerebrum...*"

"*Vincit.* What does it mean? Put crudely, it means bullshit beats brains."

THIRTEEN

A law unto themselves

I was still in bed when the phone rang. I ignored it, then my encrypted mobile rang. I scrambled around my cast off blankets and found it on the floor.

"Yep?"

"Dinny here." I was expecting Robert or Helen.

"Jeez Dinny. What time is it?"

"Early. I'm at the beach."

"You sleep there?"

"That'd be good if I could. Listen, I'm giving you a heads-up but you've got to play along. Like you don't know. OK?"

I walked to the window and opened the curtains. The morning light hit like a blast from space.

"I'll meet you at Pommie Bob's place in half an hour." Dinny said. It wasn't a request.

"Mate. I don't know exactly where Robert lives. It's in Battery Point somewhere."

Dinny sighed. "Employers nowadays. Couldn't give a stuff about their staff. 7036 Hampden Road, Flat 6. See you there. Just follow my lead, OK?"

He hung up and I staggered into the kitchen to drink enough fruit juice to start an orchard.

Dinny was waiting outside the apartment. A red tourist bus was trying to edge round his car. Chinese tourists peered out the window trying to make out whether it was Battery Point or Balmoral Beach. I was just as confused. Dinny leant against his car like they do in the movies and instructed me again in a low voice that *I should follow his bloody lead*. There was a young female cop relaxing at attention a few paces away. Her pony tail was perfect down to the last hair.

Dinny was in a dark suit with an impeccably knotted tasteful tie of yellows and greens. His shoes, as usual, were shiny as brilliantine. "You're pretty flash today, Dinny," I said

"Wife chose it," He pushed his big head towards me, "Because I was called out early, wasn't I?"

"Yeah. So was I. What's going on Dinny?"

He ignored me. In Dinny's world silence meant everything was under control but it didn't hurt to be sure.

"Dinny, nobody's been murdered in Battery point for a hundred years so is this a complaint about Robert's cooking or vacuum cleaning late at night?" I said. He nodded at the young officer who, in seconds, was standing in front of him.

"Sergeant, hand-cuff this man. Don't use your baton yet unless he tries to escape."

The young officer had the benign cute face of a horse whisperer, the type that you respected but didn't know why. She located her hand-cuffs somewhere between her pistol and taser and was about to clamp me when Dinny waved her away. I didn't want to disappoint her so I held out my hands.

Dinny lifted his eyebrows, for Dinny a massive effort, and winked at me. "Just joking Sergeant. Read the face. I keep telling you, read the face."

She looked disappointed and re-clipped the hand-cuffs onto her belt. "I *could* read your face boss but it'd take a decade." We all had a good laugh at that and then Dinny punched me hard on the arm and pointed to the outside fire-escape. The young cop hesitated before starting to follow him but Dinny said, "Go and look for pieces of that thing, that drone, up and down the street. Keep an intensive search until I call you. Don't talk to anyone." He didn't look at her but the sight of his broad back would have been enough to prove that the only good joke is the one your boss makes.

I followed him up the back stairs. We waited outside the door. From that balcony you had a great view of the port and the curved Tasman Bridge, then, to the mountains and bushland beyond the eastern shore. Two cruise ships dwarfed the port like twin Godzillas.

"What's this all about?" I repeated. I was starting to get a little nervous but I've always had this thing about cops. They do good against all odds but if, like me, you were ever a young tyke required to box three whole rounds at the Police and Citizen's Youth Clubs boxing tournaments, you got to be a bit cautious about their enthusiasms.

Dinny rang the intercom. "Yes?"

"Mr. Malahide. It's Detective Inspector Ferdinand Dinham again. Can I come in?"

I was astonished. *Ferdinand*? I had never hear him called that before. I thought, *this is serious.*

"By all means, but, I didn't do it," Robert said and laughed like a well-oiled saxophone.

Robert's apartment was a surprise. Well it was a surprise because I'd never been inside it or imagined what it would be like.

"Oh and you too." Robert said when he saw me. "I must be in trouble." He was wearing a bottle green track suit that seems to have been made out of old parachute silk.

"Nice place, Robert," I said. It was more than a nice place. It was a Georgian era show case from one end to the other. Elegant old pine table and matching chairs, silver candle sticks shaped like Corinthian columns, silk rugs on the polished board floors and, on the walls, what looked like genuine Aubusson tapestries attacked by well-bred moths. On the other walls were some of Robert's wild life shots framed in Huon Pine. I wondered if the place even had electricity.

He nodded, embarrassed. I looked around in an exaggerated manner just to make sure my own acquisitive taste was never mocked again by my staff.

"I'm paying you too much, Robert."

Robert said, "Tea?"

I said, "No" and Dinny said "No" but added briskly. "Strictly business," as if it breached Section 5 of the Police Conduct Code 2007. So I said, "Strictly business."

Robert shrugged, "Well, what can I do for you, gentlemen?" he said benignly.

Dinny drew himself up to his full height which was impressive. "Well, Mr. Malahide. Not to put too fine a point on it, someone round here is in…potentially, *significant* trouble."

Robert turned his head a little. "Ah, *trouble*." He savoured the word like a good wine. "Yes, some of my neighbours are a little…"

"Angry." Suggested Dinny in his *let me help you with your statement* voice. I would have confessed immediately but I guess Robert never went to a Police and Citizen's Youth Club.

Dinny put both hands behind his back and took a couple of paces like a London Bobby. "Yes, the kind of trouble that comes from shooting down a drone in an urban precinct. He turned to face Robert who was already in the kitchen boiling a jug, as if the problem was now mine. Dinny tried another tack, "I mean Mr. Malahide. Do you, by any chance, have a shot-gun?" He peered into the kitchen while Robert peered back out at him.

"Oh, yes. It's a family heirloom."

"Would you mind fetching it for me?" The politeness was becoming intimidating.

Robert shrugged and went into the other room. Whilst he was gone, Dinny turned and moved quickly to the balcony. I followed him out. He scanned the area around a Turkish pot filled with red geraniums. He touched something with his foot, turning it over delicately. It was the mangled part remains of a drone exposed like a dead eagle on the balcony tiles.

"Hmm." Dinny said and looked at me curiously until Robert returned with a leather and oak case. He held it out to Dinny with both hands.

"Not here. Inside," Dinny said looking around.

Robert took the case inside and offered it to Dinny.

"Open it please."

Robert opened the case.

"Give it me please."

Robert took the shot-gun out and handed it over carefully, even lovingly. The artistically carved wooden stock and the inlaid silver workings shone in the morning sun. Dinny turned it over in his hands. For a moment there was a touch of reverence and a faint smile,

"Well, well. A Prudey HC," He turned it over. "HC, 0180/9 I think."

"Purdey." Robert said quietly.

Dinny gave him the look that detectives reserve for Moors Murderers.

"Prudey." He said firmly. "That's what I said."

He turned it over again." Single trigger, over and under game gun. Gold inlay cocking indicators. Been beautifully maintained. So clean you could have sworn it'd been cleaned only yesterday.

"Which it wasn't." Robert said quickly.

"Wasn't what?"

"Uhm, cleaned yesterday".

Dinny broke open the barrels and looked down them intently, squinting.

"Family heirloom. That why you don't have a licence?"

The kettle was whistling and Robert sprinted to the kitchen where he took his time filling a Meissen ware teapot which he immediately covered with a tea caddy. "Sure you don't want tea? Yes. I guess it is a family heirloom. Yes, an heirloom."

Dinny smiled and closed the barrels. "Yep. Family heirloom. Elizabethan."

Robert looked puzzled as Dinny handed it back," Elizabeth the Second I reckon. Best clean it again. Don't use that WD40 oil. Scours. It scours. And...when you've done that, present it to the Museum for safekeeping."

He sauntered out onto the balcony where he took in the view, squinting into the morning vista of sun, blue cloud-scudding skies and wide river. He sniffed appreciatively.

"Yep. Whoever shot that those bloody things down deserves a medal. They'll be delivering coffee and burgers in them next. And I ask you, where would we be then, eh?" He paused to look us over. "See ya."

He motioned me to stay and finish the unfinished business. We could hear him whistling like the Third Man as he plodded down the stairs.

I turned to Robert, "I'll have that cup of tea, now." I sat at the dining table and pulled out my mobile but I was really admiring the apartment. A speck of dust would have looked like a boulder.

"You know, I've never been invited here. Table manners not up to scratch?"

Robert knew where I was going. He eyed me warily as he poured the tea but he was so nervous you could hear the spout tapping the cup. I thought he was going to break down and tell me about Winchester or whichever rugger-bugger posh boy school his parents exiled him to. You could almost smell the aura of stale dining halls and gowns and freezing dormitories that turn out real men and frightened boys.

I pointed at one of the photographs on the wall. A lion was leaping at an Impala. The shot had been taken a split second before the actual impact, a moment in time between life and death.

"That is stunning. You must have exposed yourself to danger getting those shots."

He passed me the cup and saucer as if it contained an explosive device. "You are cautious but you're excited and free. Alert but you are free in that world. You take risks but it's inordinately preferable to the way...humans prey on each other and they oppress each other and that is crueller than..." He paused, surprised at his own nervous outburst.

"Than what?" I said.

"Than killing to survive." He said and suddenly stared at the photograph deep in thought. I was still angry about his carelessness and I was not going to let him off the hook.

"Yes, survival and discretion." I said quietly.

"Discretion. Yes. I'm afraid old man, I might have been momentarily...unbalanced."

"Unbalanced?"

"With anger."

I sipped the tea. It was what the doctor ordered when you are trying to remain calm. I looked at the other framed photos on the wall. Apart from the stunning photography with its light variations, all shared the same theme, animals before or after the kill.

"Robert. You have just warned *Coming Now* that we are onto them. Just one little problem you've created. Look mate. We are trying hard to stay inside their tent and I want to get another one hundred grand out of them. You don't want to work for them, Helen doesn't want to work for them and I bloody don't want to work for them. We're spying on them. They're spying on us. What kind of business relationship is that? But we've got to soldier on. You have now made it that much harder."

"Yes" Robert said quietly. He was now sitting on the sofa, the settee or whatever his family called it. His arms dangled like a rag doll on a wet day. To this day I cannot forget that face which had suddenly grown ten years older. He lifted his tired head. "What can I do?"

"Keep spying. That's what you do. Keep spying."

Speaking of discretion when I went to lunch, Donna was still blushing. She also avoided my eyes with a grim determination.

"Donna, what's up?"

"You know very well, Mr. Kennedy. It's not right, that's all I have to say."

"Of course it's not right. They shouldn't have."

FOURTEEN

The swallow, a nest for itself

Some weekends are better than others. Some are just different, like that one. I retreated to the shack in Primrose Sands. I was trying to solve the big issues of the week. I had leaks that had already dripped water into one of my bookshelves and the stone wall that had done my back in still looked decidedly wobbly. But the day was brisk and clear and the islands floated like magic across the bay.

I walked around a lot to think about where I could place another water tank without making the whole place look like Ma and Pa Kettle's cabin. Three kangaroos stared arrogantly at me from the vacant block next door while rosellas squawked and bullied the wattle birds and magpies. There was a fake smell of autumn and wood fires in the air.

Later, I had another go at rebuilding the stone wall. Robert Frost said something about good walls making good neighbours. My neighbours thought I was nuts. *Paling fences, mate, paling fences.* I was soon lifting and placing stones and digging foundation channels, concentrating to make sure each stone was laid correctly. In Frost's New England it was said that farmers could keep a picture of the final rock wall pattern in their minds as they laid the stone to fit tightly. Those wiseacres had obviously never been to Primrose Sands that autumn.

I was pondering this and other momentous philosophies when I felt a light touch on the shoulder.

"God almighty! You almost gave me the last rites!" I said. It was Helen looking a little stunned and shy. And beautiful too with her red hair done severely in a bun.

"Sorry, I didn't mean to startle you."

"Startle me. No. I'm just surprised. You've never been here before."

"Yes, the other day."

"That doesn't count. You swore black and blue you would never come to my place or my places to be more exact."

She smiled so those lovely fine lines either side of her mouth surfaced again. "Can't a maiden change her mind about her man?"

"A maiden can certainly change her mind about her man."

"I like your rock work," She said.

"It's not rock. It's stone."

She laughed and put her Blundstones against the wall I had just re-laid. She leaned and pushed until the top layer then the next fell over, then laughed even louder.

"What the hell did you do that for?'

"Because, that is a badly laid rock wall. It's a danger to dogs and children. What've you done to your hand?"

She pulled my hand towards her and started to prod the swollen area where my finger was already turning blue. I had an inheritance from my father, not likeTommy Rayfinger's money or school tie. My heritage was impatience and total incapacity to drive a nail straight or place a stone without dislocating a finger or two.

"Look over there, "she said and pulled my dislocated finger hard enough to put it back in place.

"That bloody hurt!" I shouted and nursed my hand. "You've never been here before and, in five bloody minutes, you've given me a heart attack and a finger that couldn't order a beer. You know, you could go and burn the place down, just to finish my life off."

She ambled up the slope and surveyed the shack with a critical eye, peering at the rusty spouting and the peeling paint. The old crayfish pots didn't seem so charming now and the fly-wire door needed a bit of love and affection. She stood at the top of the veranda steps and absently swung the hammock.

"Am I allowed inside? Or is it boys only in there? I dread to think."

"You, you are here on sufferance. You are a first time visitor so behave yourself."

"Does a girl get a beer round here?" She said and walked straight inside.

I could hear her say, "Ooh! Ah! Abattoir!"

I followed her in. "Well, I've been working." I explained.

She looked around, walked to the fridge, opened it and waved her long fingers in front of her face. "Is that dinosaur meat?"

Nevertheless, she took out two beers and opened them on each other like a professional or maybe she wasn't too keen on using my glasses.

"So," I said. "This *is* a treat! If I had known you were coming, I would have baked a cake."

She looked around the lounge room with its second hand furniture, fishing rods stacked against the pine wood walls and lack of curtains.

"I wouldn't have eaten it." She took a swig of the beer and peered into the bedroom. "Woo hoo! You've made your bed. Good boy! We might need it later."

"Don't kid yourself. You've got to be invited".

"You'll be grateful." She lifted her green eyes.

She started opening cupboards and fingered for dust. The bookshelves were thoroughly examined and the bathroom inspected.

"I hope all those books aren't up there in your brain."

"If they have a date and a signature in them, then it means I read them. Incidentally, there wasn't a book in your house, anywhere."

"That's because I read e-books."

"Yeah, like what?"

She pursed her lips. "Like, let me think. Yep. Like *The Psychology of Drones* by Werner von Braun."

"You are taking the Mickey?"

"Yep. So, you're wondering why I came here."

"Not wondering," I said, "I'm astonished."

She went to the big glass window that looked out over the bay and the islands. A light breeze was riffing the water which broke on the rocks and tall lonely gums played in the air while she-oaks clung to the rocky slopes like country cousins.

"Would you like to take a shower?" She said, then paused to show that it wasn't an instruction. "Together if you like?"

I couldn't stop laughing. One minute, I'm lugging stones and placing them in position, the next I was trying to lift Helen in the shower so that we could fit together like a well-made wall. It was one of those surprises of middle age lovers or at least one middle aged lover and his maiden as Helen called it. The water cascaded and hands explored smooth bodies and wet hair, kissing and laughing and not laughing and moving like dance partners. Clothes were strewn all over the floor from the main room to the shower entrance and stayed there until we slept a little while later on the bed.

"I will never ask you what caused this turn-around." I said as we lay folded together on the bed.

"No, you wouldn't. Because I'll never tell you."

It was a good way to spend a Summer Saturday. Comfortable. Not talking until Helen stood and started picking up her clothes and dressing. I liked the totally unself-conscious way she dressed herself, as if her army life had made her just another person with a job to do and places to go. Her hips always seemed to fit easily into those regulation tank pants she often wore. One shrug and lift then one button and zip. Her still wet hair had stopped clinging to her freckled back and now was shaken so that it hung like a cascade of copper. She retrieved her white T-shirt and started pulling it over her bare pink breasts. She looked curiously at me.

"What?"

"Nothing, you know I'm a little bit in..." I started.

She held her finger up, warning, "Don't say it. Ok?" She was in earnest and I knew exactly what she meant. Then she brightened again.

"So, what's for lunch?" she said.

"La Cuisine de Primmy will be open soon. Would Mademoiselle care to partake of a little salade with a disgusting arrangement of prawns, scallops, cucumber, tomato, olives, peppers, garlic, pitta bread and humus? "

"You're an idiot."

"But a good cook. There's a couple of bottles of white in the fridge. Pick the Pooleys Chardonnay."

She went to the fridge. "Today is the first day of my la-de-da life. There's a song there, you know." She chose two glasses and huffed into them like she was cleaning spectacles.

"That is disgusting," I said.

She turned and filled the glasses, shaking her head slowly with mock horror "Disgusting? You have just done some indescribably intimate things with me and now you object to me huffing your glass. Jeez, Louise"

We bumped into each in the small kitchen, cutting tomatoes and bread and laying out cheeses. The bread still had that fresh baked sweet smell that makes you want to break it and dip it in the basil pesto and hummus all at once then lick your fingers as well.

We played with the anchovies and sat back with our wine.

Helen reached over and broke off more bread. For a relatively slim woman she had a prodigious appetite and ate quickly.

"Eat!" She commanded through a mouthful of bread dipped in the anchovies.

"I am eating but I know that there will be a tomorrow so I'll eat slowly," Then I regretted it immediately. She shrugged and studied me, one hand holding the bread.

"You're an idiot. But you are forgiven and I will talk to you later about *some things*"

"Only if you want to."

"Well I can tell you something now. That bloody telephone freak is from my old unit and...do you really want to hear this?"

"Of course I do."

She wiped her hands on the table napkin and took a sip of the wine. "Now I don't want you to say anything, ok? And I'll say it once and never mention it again. OK?"

"OK."

"Well he was in my unit. We did tours of the Ghan and Iraq together. He and another bloke. You understand that, in those units, we are very tight. Just like that." She put her thumb and index finger together, "We were pretty front line; well, very front line. As you know, in fact there's no such thing as a front line. When a twelve year kid can offer tea and blows himself and you to smithereens, there can't be a front line.

We had a special role which included locating insurgents. I mean big time insurgents, ones that had technical skills and needed neutralizing. We acted on other intel and moved forward to gather the co-ordinates and guide our air strikes or drones to hit those bad guys."

She pursed her lips. There was a momentary tremor then she continued.

"Well, not to put too fine a point on it, one time, we fucked up."

"How?" I had a fair idea what that meant.

"We caused collateral damage as they put it. Civilians. Kids, mothers. No-one to blame but all of us to blame. I'm not going to go into exactly what happened, but the result was an unofficial inquiry. This was front line stuff so it couldn't be public or official. Well, I told the truth. No cover-ups. Not my nature. I didn't blab. I just answered what I was asked. The other two didn't answer truthfully and one still carries it around like a bloody Arab vendetta. And he is bloody dangerous and it's like he learned something over there..."

"What's that?"

"That you take revenge on your enemy's friends first. To make the threat more compelling. That's why when he phones, his message is always like that. Friends first, then you."

One minute we had been happy and laughing and making love. The next we were sitting round a table and the day was changing fast. Helen hadn't taken her eyes off me, as if wanting to register my every reaction. Somewhere in the distance a chain saw barked and whined and the line of 4WDs with boats on trailers headed away from the ramp. Then she straightened her shoulders as if she were on parade somewhere in the bleak barren hills again.

"OK." She said.

"Look, if you want to..." I started.

She waved her hands like those TV basketball referees. Firm and no arguments. "Enough. Absolutely enough. Where's the coffee? I want to tell you about *Coming Now*. We've got the polling results."

I was still thinking about Iraq and Afghanistan and that crazy phone call I'd heard on Helen's phone. "Ok. Where's the report?" I said without much enthusiasm.

"I didn't bring the written report. You can have a copy later after we tidy up the demographic profiles. So, this is the situation. We polled two thousand in that electorate and then weighted them at a higher than usual rate to account for a fifty-fifty split between land line and mobile phones. That gives us a better representation of younger people than most of the cheaper polling."

"Are you ok?" I interrupted. She pouted her lips a little and lifted her head.

"Yes. I am ok. Now, as I was saying," She peered sternly at me. "What the focus groups said doesn't stack up. Too many of them put on their angel haloes when they're face to face with strangers, as you well know. Get 'em on the phone, they become right royal little racists. Middle class hides it better but they still think the same. Don't like foreigners controlling our jobs, land and resources. They mean China of course. They're not particularly religious but they don't like Muslims and so and so on."

I was still eying her warily. "That answers two of *Coming Now's* questions. Skip the other stuff. I can look at it Monday. What do the polls say about Pastor Tommy's primary vote?"

She laughed, "You remember how we laughed about his crazy ambitions, all of them?"

"I didn't."

She made a face and moved her head side to side like a carnival clown. "True. You did not. We all thought Tammy and Tommy were nuts. Well, these polls show he has sky high recognition and, get this, he would win the seat easily. If he spends big time."

I sat back. When we weren't trying to find out what was behind the *Coming Now* team, we'd been doing a lot of work that was obviously paying off for Tommy. We had advised the *Coming Now* team to get out brochures, slides in cinemas, videos and social media even before he was preselected. All of it intended to persuade the preselectors that Tommy would win the seat in a canter. All standard stuff emphasizing Tommy's charity work and youth programs (stripped of their religious connotations), pretty pictures but with lucerne fields rather than wheat fields behind the happy family, Pastor Tommy with school kids and old people, that kind of thing plus our phone campaign. It was working. The *Coming Now* team was getting value for money and, in return, we were getting the guilts.

"Proves that having the money and the resources does work." I said. *Winning a Grand Final knowing that you had cheated, your client spying on you and you spying back, wondering why you were putting another bible bashing salesman on the green leather seats. A nice week's work.*

"Remind me to ask for that extra one hundred grand on Monday." I said.

She tapped me on the shoulder. "Greed is the root of all evil," she said. "Robert is really unearthing a lot of stuff about *Coming Now.* Like what he calls the resourcing issue, meaning all their assets and connections"

"How's he going?"

"He says it is a minefield and that accounts for the way they are sticking so resolutely to their own grand program. It explains why Pastor Tommy caved into his funeral team. *Coming Now* is bigger than we ever imagined and a lot better organised. That's what Robert says. What are you staring at?"

"Your green eyes."

"Well don't. It's bad luck. Want to go for a walk?"

"Sure. You know, when I'm down here, I do actually switch off from work but that means I get to thinking why we work for such tossers. We wouldn't vote for Tommy Rayfinger in a fit yet, here we are putting lipstick on that particular pig. Anyway we can look at Robert's report on Monday. Secure, out of the office."

We walked along the road to the beach. The waves were being driven from the South-West but the air was warm and there had been a pod of dolphins in the shallows that morning, looping in sympathy with each other.

The beach was full of kids splashing and optimistically building sandcastles with moats, harbouring secret thoughts about the destruction as walls collapsed and the beach returned to itself. You're supposed to say *that's life* or something from the sages but all I could remember was the time when we were kids ourselves at this very beach. Cricket and swimming all summer, burnt to a crisp by the fierce sun, wearing Buck Rogers space suits straight from the Christmas stockings. Hot sand on your bare feet and fires on the beaches with the first sexual stirrings. And my old man's tinny, slap slapping the greenish waters as I watched them become disturbingly deeper beneath the boat.

"Why didn't the French stay?" Helen said. She snuggled closer even though the air was mild. "I mean, didn't they come here, and down there at Bruny and Recherche Bay?"

"They were everywhere. I read the journals of Nicolas Baudin once. There was a Revolution in France while they were on the other side of the world and they had shit fights between the Monarchists and Republicans on Baudin's own ship. And anyway, they didn't think they had a right to hoist their flag and take possession. You know, they had these Enlightenment ideas about native people's being entitled to first possession or whatever they called it."

She tugged at my sleeve and put her arms inside mine. "Tommy Know-All." She said and pecked me on the cheek. There were kids coming out of the shop. A couple of them giggled then started demolishing their chocolate ice-creams with artistic fervour, turning them around to get a better lick.

"You know, we could give it all up. Write ice-cream and pie

jingles. Never have to work for people like the Rayfingers ever again." Helen said then paused and clapped her hands together mockingly. "Oh. I forgot, you *have already* written classics yourself. *The Tassie Pie song.* Who could forget that? The John Lennon of the pie world." She laughed like a drain and started singing the *Tassie Pie song*. She had a nice pure voice which still didn't make the joke any better. The ice-cream kids giggled again and tip-toed on the hot sand in the dunes.

> *"Tassie Pies, they hit the spot*
> *In times of trouble they never lie*
> *Hit the spot, got the lot*
> *Good old Tassie Pie*
> *Good old, good old Tassie Pie."*

She remembered every word, which wasn't a surprise. She could recite formulae and manuals and demographic detail without notes so, the little old *Tassie Pie song* would have been a push-over.

Late in the afternoon we wandered back along the track that meandered between the she-oaks and the easy sea thumping gently on the rocks below. In the lone gum trees and in the settling sky, hooligan white cockatoos seemed to be disputing the correctness of Hegel or Heidegger, leaving the swallows to flit and chirrup in the currents below. It was a good evening to live the Tassie dream of shack, boat and sea.

We ate almost in contented silence on the balcony, watching the islands and the wooded peninsulars gradually disappearing in the long descent of the sun.

I played some Handel and, for once, she did not complain. The music soon ran out and we let the soft sound of evening become the music.

"I like it that you are a sentimental sook. I bet you cry at operas.

Well, I bet you actually go to operas."

"Yep. I do. That song I just played. Handel's *Largo*. They used to play that on the local radio station when they announced a death. *It is with deep regret that we announce the death of Fred Jensch, dearly beloved husband of...*and so on. And they played Handel's *Largo*. I always thought it was just beautiful. Yeah, I'm a sook. And you know what? My grandmother who was a music teacher, when I told her I love Handel's *Largo*, I couldn't have been more than nine years old, she said, it's a beautiful piece of music but they're wasting it on funeral announcements. That's the kind of treatment we sentimental sooks get. Wasted on funerals!"

Helen put her feet on the other chair. "Rub my back. Just there. You know, all I had was Country and Western. *Stand by Your Man, Don't it Make Your Brown Eyes Blue* et cetera and oh, then the heavy metal that my mates in the services played all the time. It was a sort of madness, bang, bang, bang! It took me a long time to learn to listen to music though a lot of people seem to get through life living the music, if you know what I mean.'

"Your turn to make the bed." I said. The night was finally settling and the cockatoos had solved their dispute about Hegel and Heidegger. A light breeze shook the trees and lights were going out in the shacks. Locals in their baggy shorts and T-shirts generally followed the pattern of the day, waking at sun-rise, going to bed when the Southern light finally failed about ten o'clock.

"I've already made it, "she said.

The night was still warm so we lay naked and listened to the possums scurry and bicker competing with the shishing of the waves. Out there it was still possible to imagine the soft footfall of the aborigines who once came to the bay to hunt, fish and wait.

The phone rang. I checked my heart rate then answered it.

"It's Robert. I'm sorry old man to wake you at this hour."

"I wasn't sleeping. I was …" Helen gave me a kick in the back. "I was contemplating."

"Yes. Awfully sorry but there's something you ought to know, if you are in contact with our friends from *Coming Now.*"

"Robert. It's ten o'clock. Are you still working?"

"I've finished now. This won't take long. The long and short of it is that *Coming Now* is big, awfully big."

"Yeah, we were getting that impression."

"No, big as big can be."

"That big?"

He seemed terse. "No. To give you the picture in a nutshell, since you are probably busy. You know the development application for the warehouse distribution centre in Sorell? Well, there are seventeen other applications in. And they're in all the marginal electorates around the country. All of them. And, even more striking, old man, is the fact that another twenty have been approved already and are currently operating, judging by their accounts I saw."

I whistled. "Now that is big, big. Are you absolutely sure?"

"I am certain. I followed the fees trail, you know the bank statements indicate local government fees then there is their budget for the construction. It all adds up and there have been payments made on all the approved projects."

"That is a lot of dough. Of course it's an attempt to win support from his soon to be colleagues in those electorates. But it's a greater game than that." I said. Helen was very close to me, listening. In the moonlight, her skin was glistening.

"That is not all. There's more. I've analysed the business plan. These are not just your common a garden warehouses. They are designed to be office space, for local business, particularly small businesses, at what looks like substantially discounted rents."

"*Coming Now.* The next retail giant, helping small business get bigger. There's a slogan and business in that, for us." I said.

Robert sniffed. "And there is more. Those distribution centres will use drones to carry everything, coffee and fast food, parcels to be delivered to shops and cafes…"

It was late. "Robert. Is there more?"

"More, oh more indeed! The business plan specifically states that the concept is delivery everywhere, any time. You see, the problem with traditional truck or courier delivery for anything you order online is that people often aren't home. It's a big conundrum. So *Coming Now* will deliver to cafes, small shops, whichever place the customer nominates. The customer picks it up at their leisure. It makes cafes, coffee shops, newsagents all collection points. It also allows them and *Coming Now* to build a very big data base for all their customers, especially valuable in marginal seats. Clever, eh?"

"Very clever. Anything else?"

"Yes, old man. They are buying land on behalf of non-Australians who would otherwise have needed permission from the Foreign Investment Review Board. Now there is one thing that bothers me and I can't make head nor tale of it. The revenues go to a trust account."

"Where?"

"South Dakota. Can you believe it? Some bucolic little Mid-West state. No one in *Coming Now* has any connection with that state. South Dakota. That's where the trail just peters out."

I was intrigued but Robert's enthusiasm was enough for a late Sunday night. Then it struck me. "Robert, where are you now?"

"I'm in…I'm in the office."

"Robert. Get off the bloody phone, leave the office immediately!" I almost shouted.

Outside the wind was whipping up and the night birds were warning each other about danger and checking for intruders that crawled or hunted in the darkness.

The first step in the defrocking of Tommy Rayfinger was the radio talk show in Hobart. Aim? To show that Tommy Rayfinger was thoughtful and basically a good bloke and hardly a Pastor at all. The deep voice was made for radio and Tommy, once he was out of sight of the religious crows like Lieutenant Squeaky and Brother Underwood, took to it like a duck to water.

"Chris. You asked why the new anti-discrimination laws will let employers hire and fire employees if those employees don't conform to the employer's religious views. Right?"

"Right."

"Well, look at it this way. What employer in their right mind would want to fire a good employee if that employee is doing a good job? Just doesn't make sense."

"Tommy Rayfinger, can I raise that hoary old chestnut about the religious baker and his wife who won't bake a wedding cake for a gay wedding because homosexuality offends the baker's religious views? Where do you stand on that?"

"That's simple, Chris. The new Federal Government bill respects the baker's right to freedom of expression. It also respects the homosexual couple's right to take their business to another baker. It's like a football club…"

"With which Pastor Tommy, you have had significant experience.'

"Yes, not as tragic as your experiences with Essendon but then we only ever won one premiership at St. Kilda. So, I shouldn't gloat. Like a football club or a netball club you don't have to join them. You're free to join another club or play another sport. It's all about freedom of choice, isn't it?"

Robert got up from his chair and poured a lemon juice for Helen and me. Lately he'd been on this health kick with Helen who already had her own home gym which sat out in the vegetable garden hacked out in a clearing between the trees and the river. *Robert's True Conversion* as Helen called it. No tea or coffee, no lunch time pastries. And, Robert had joined the city gym where Helen worked out every day. *He's a bloody fanatic, is our Robert. Chin-ups, bench presses. He beats me and he never gives up.*

Robert Malahide was also very professional. He had no time for slick salesmen like Tommy Rayfinger who he regarded as self-promoting ignoramuses. But, he beavered away on the promotional material as if Tommy had founded a foster home for refugee kids. Yes, professional in every sense except for one thing. Robert Malahide was in my club when it came to mawkish teenage lyrics and strumming guitars. *Jesus saved us all with his blood and you'd better watch out kid because the devil will get you and I hope I'm saved, treat me right and make me whole. Islam has haunting music and calls to prayer but you'd also better watch out, the armies of the Lord are coming.*

The radio host and Tommy were still carefully testing each other out. Tommy was on a roll.

"Yes, Chris. *Coming Now Deliveries* is a business. We aim to use new technologies to make our society more efficient. And I'm a businessman. And I'll tell you what my aim as a businessman is. My wife Tammy and I want every young person to get a decent job, especially in new industries. To reward those that have a go. They're the ones who get a go. That's the aim of Tammy and me because we are in this together. Nothing more important than families. Call me old fashioned but it's family, first, second and third."

"Pastor Tommy Rayfinger..."

"Just plain Tommy is fine."

"Just one other thing, briefly. How's the housing challenge going?"

"It's going just fine and dandy. We've got three other business people who've already pledged to match my offer. A lot of families are going to have a roof over their heads by the end of this year."

"Tommy Rayfinger. Thank you for coming on. Up next, which cemeteries have been saved from Church sales? Is the fight to save churches from sale splitting the Anglican Church?"

"OK," I said to Robert and Helen. "Happy with that? Was he on message? The pre-selectors going to like that? OK Robert, put that out on Tommy's blog and Facebook page. Oh and on Twitter."

"He runs his own Twitter account." Robert said abruptly.

"Robert. Tell me you love working for this pumpkin." Helen said and touched him on the end of his Patrician nose.

Robert rolled his eyes ever so slightly, cracked a reluctant smile and went off to knock out the social media releases. *Well done thy good and faithful servant.*

I held my nose and texted Tommy's phone. *Well done.* It was the best I could do but getting Tommy away from the religious crows was a step in the right direction. Either that or an act of folly.

FIFTEEN

Lips of a strange woman

"I reckon they all bloody lie and they're in it for themselves. That's what I think." Colin was not going to let the facts get in the way of a strong opinion. Twelve good Tasmanians and true sitting around a covered BBQ area waiting for the Weber to warm up and Colin to finish mansplaining.

It was another great way to spend a Monday evening. A one hour focus group to finish the series we were delivering to *Coming Now*.

Focus groups are meant to provide politicians with the true views of the Australian population. In-depth questioning by experts builds a picture of how Aussie Man and Woman thinks about the issues of the day and, of course, how they feel about the politicians paying for the little gatherings that are occurring all over the country in hotels, church halls or wherever. It's a ritual which allows the political class to refine their responses and slogans to get them over the line at election time or to convince their colleagues to dump a leader.

The other option, if you want to run the country, is to own media outlets or spend sixty million dollars pummeling your poorer opponents into the election dust.

That evening was like any other but at least it was the end of a long road. Fifteen focus groups in different parts of Tassie. It was like reading the same chapter of a novel over and over and each tribe was writing in a different language. Edith, the psychologist we hired to do the final focus group was polite, well dressed in comfortable shoes, a tartan skirt with a large pin, a neat no-nonsense blouse and a demeanour to match.

"Yes." She said, "I'm hearing you. Are others disappointed with the standard of our elected representatives?" She had that purry consoling voice that could make cancer sound a blessing. *Next time I must hire a truck driver to run a group and we'll fill them full of beer and really find out what they think.*

A woman who described herself as a housewife fidgeted with her hands and spoke too loudly as nervous people often do. She stopped and cleared her throat.

"I really think that perhaps they just have some very bad advisors. You know, advisors, those people you don't elect who haven't really actually done anything...in sort of life..." She broke off as if she had run out of adrenaline. *Keep going luv, you're correctisimo about those thin tied, tight panted advisors and the mad ones who come off the Think Tank assembly line like gum-nut babies looking for power and adventure and the right to push ordinary folks around.*

"So, can I run some names past you?" Edith said. She was reading virtually from the script and probably would have preferred to be more subtle but this was a BBQ focus group not a Freudian psychotherapy session and our fees were less. "Just tell me what comes to mind when you hear them. Tommy Rayfinger. Anyone know him and what do you think about him?"

"He's the St. Kilda fullback." Colin said.

"He's a businessman who helps people get houses." Brianna said. She was in her twenties and harassed by a toddler who kept pushing his weight against her legs, insistently.

"He was gonna make it big time but he didn't have what it takes to make it over there," Colin added helpfully. *Thanks Colin, you've still got the Tassie cringe. Couldn't make it over there. We're not even good enough to push and shove the Victorian suits to get our own AFL footy team. We've got writers and artists and anyone who's still here can't be any good whereas, in Sydney on the Mainland, jeez, they're competitive over there and if Scomo, our Prime Minister, so much as visits Tassie's North and Northwest and eats a sausage in public we're bloody grateful. And if that Rayfinger thinks he can be Prime Minister he'll fall flat on his arse, mark my words. And if the Chinese are smart enough to buy up all the best agricultural land and city real estate then good on them. And I'm a businessman and I know we need overseas investment. All the best Tasmanian assets, yes, we need the investment.*

There was a text on my old phone. It was from Tammy Rayfinger. *Am on East Coast. Call me to meet. Just you and me.* I texted back and we agreed to meet later that evening near Scamander, the holiday town an hour away. The directions were precise. A run down farm with a *No Trespassing* sign at the gate. For the *Coming Now* mob, the *No Trespassing* was a nice touch.

I left our facilitator to finish the job of drilling into Tasmania's psyche and headed for the door.

"The trouble with Labor is it's in, you know, in bed with the Greens, like climate change." The small businessman in reefer jacket and fawn chinos was back to his old theme. The attractive smell of the barbeque drifted into the warm air but it needs a miracle worker to eat a chop on a paper plate with impunity and I figured I could eat on the way.

Helen had gone back to Hobart to work through the material with Robert so I opened the window and sucked in the scent of wattles and gums in the winding sections of the St. Mary's Pass. There were few other cars on the road and I thought about Helen and the changes that had come over her lately. I was being let into her world one step at a time. It made me edgy but as excited as anyone closing on forty could be. I turned the radio off and just listened to the hiss of tyres and exhaust noise pirouetting in the dense tree canopy and man-ferns in the steep gulleys below.

I stopped at a road side café, filled the tank and had a coffee that was good. A scallop pie was on the menu with my name on it.

The waitress was about forty but a little careworn. She watched me demolish the pie.

"Local." She said as if it was the next star after four star Michelin.

"I like local," I said.

"How's your day been so far?" She put a sticky sugar bowl in front of me.

"As good as it gets." I said thinking about my meeting with Tammy Rayfinger.

"Well, you're a lucky boy." She said neutrally as if her day was about to head down-hill from there.

It was still light by the time I reached the *No Trespassing* sign. It was more than a sign, it was a billboard with *Strictly No Access* in bright red letters across the face for those who, like some of our focus group, didn't believe what they read.

Tammy Rayfinger was standing alongside a large black customised Ford pick-up truck, chromed bars on the tray and bull bars. Standing to one side like a White House security guard was Brother Underwood. He was wearing the same dark suit as if the effort to undress from his well-toned bulk would have required a chainsaw.

"I thought we were going to meet alone," I said.

She didn't look at Underwood. "We are." She said, "A few bad things have happened on this road so a girl wouldn't want to be on her own." She tossed her head slightly and Underwood went for a walk to talk to the kangaroos.

"No, a girl wouldn't." I said.

She flicked her well coiffured head again and said. "We can sit in the vehicle while we talk." It was a direction not a request. I opened the door and she lifted herself into the behemoth like a high school athlete, exposing shapely legs that would have done credit to any cheer leader or pom-pom girl. The cabin was an explosion of very expensive perfume and white leather upholstery.

"So." I said.

"So. Let me very frank," She said and wound the window down. "Can I smoke?"

"Sure." I said, trying to find the electric window control on my side.

She took out a leather cigarette holder. White like the upholstery.

"Matching ensemble?" I said.

She exhaled expressively. I expected perfectly formed smoke rings to come out of her immaculate painted red lips.

"Yes. Came with the vehicle honey. I only smoke when I'm upset and, to be honest with you, I'm a little upset right now." She turned and looked me full in the eyes, long enough for me to take in a long lingering view of mascara and longer than life lashes.

I stared at the vista across the road. Farmland pasture and crops rolled all the way down to the sea. Night was coming in but the light picked out the hills and capes like a sepia print.

"Yes, honey. Lately, I've been thinking that things haven't been going along so well between us and we oughta do something about that little problem. Don'tcha think?"

I turned to her. "Yep. You could start by accepting some of our advice. Instead, it's like you're adopting everything your little and big advisors say."

"They've been with us a long time. Honey, we listen but you gotta understand that we got this mission, this plan and it's been around a long time, that plan has. Also you gotta admit that we pay you guys well and there's another one hundred grand already in your account today. No traceable cheques this time. Spect you'd like that."

"We like that. Thank you."

"You know, Pastor Tommy is also getting a little restless."

"He's got candidate disease. Makes them edgy." I said.

"Patrick. My husband is an action man but you know something? He's a real man in every way. And handsome. When they held the genetic lottery, Tommy was way out there in front. But, he's also deprived. Yep, a deprived personality." She elongated the word.

"Deprived? That's not a word I'd associate with Tommy." I said.

Before I knew it she had placed her manicured hands on my knee. I didn't move. "Yes. He's not like you and me. You and me, we're fighters, we had nothing, maybe a loving family, that's all. I can tell that it's the same with you. Plain as day. My family was everything and, you'd better believe it, my kids are everything now. Whatever happens, any time, anywhere. You understand me?"

She fixed me with her big eyes, suddenly grown fiercer.

"Sure, I get you." I said and thought a little about my ex-wife, a long time ago, saying the same thing. But, somewhere, for all his bullshit and unseemliness as my mother used to say, at least Tommy Rayfinger wasn't going to be pulled down by the Tasmanian Cringe. It was PM or nothing. Trouble was, it was very easy to go from hero to zero in two seconds flat so maybe that's why Tommy and his kind need a woman like Tammy who couldn't spell words like zero or modest ambition if her life depended on it.

"Now, Tommy is different. Got sent to boarding school when he was only a little runt, at *seven* years old. Boarding school! And he lived in the same town, just four kilometres away! I mean, seriously. Then he got picked up in the football draft and he worked at it, just like he worked at everything he does. Then he got serious money and fame in that football world. Too much, too soon. Sure he started with money but he didn't have what you and I have."

"Which is what?" I said. There we were on the side of the highway isolated from the rest of the world and we were discussing Pastor Tommy Rayfinger's deprived childhood while a religious security guard patrolled the perimeter looking for kangaroos.

She smiled and withdrew her hand, "Which is a core, honey. A core that keeps you being what you are. Nobody gonna push you around, ever."

She took out her phone and scrolled through some photographs then held it towards me. It featured a deserted run down country church that was vaguely familiar.

"What's that?" I said.

"Honey. That was our very first little old church. Up for sale it was and I said to Tommy, this is what the Good Lord has given us. This is where your Ministry starts and it's gonna be the place where we're gonna start climbing and..."

"Tammy."

She waved her long thin hands and threw her cigarette out the window, maybe to test the local bush fire brigade.

"I know. Honey. You wanna know what this is all about. Well, since you know so much about us, we got a bond, right?"

"Correct. A bond." I lied.

"Well, a bond is usually based on some sharing and that means sharing of the rewards. Huh?"

"I'd say another hundred grand is a mighty good reward." I said.

Tammy snorted. "Oh fiddle fuddle! You aint seen nothing yet. When I say rewards, I mean real rewards, not dill pickle." Her Deep South roots were starting to emerge the further she got into her narrative. And I sensed her narrative *was* going somewhere, somewhere interesting or just plain dangerous; that would explain what Robert had told me yesterday evening and now this strange meeting as Brother Underwood prowled outside in the dark like Simon Legree.

"You wouldn't want dill pickle." I said and meant it.

"Yessiree, you want the rewards. Now we got two ambitions. One is to make my husband the next Prime Minister. The other is to make *Coming Now* a mighty big corporation that's gonna be there for ever and ever. Don't care which. Both if that's possible."

"For ever and ever...until the End of Days."

She looked suspiciously at me in the gathering dark. "Yuh. And that too."

I was thinking about Robert's information. It was worth a try.

"So, where do we come in, apart from the PM thing?" I said.

A car went past on the highway and honked its horn. It was a reminder of where we were that Monday night.

"OK." I said, "We know you've got a lot of investments all over the place. And that's your private business but what's with the land investments? Does it create any political problems that we might need to head off at the pass?"

She pressed a button and the electric windows whirred and closed. She leant forward so close I could smell the cigarette on her breath and the lingering scent of her perfume. It wasn't unpleasant, in fact, there was a sense of excitement.

"Honey, see that land across the road. That's ours, that's just a teensy weensy part of the plan and there's a lotta other places like that just waiting to be gobbled up. Just gobbled up, like that. But it's gonna need some law changing to make it happen and that's where you guys come in. And when that happens, you my friend, get a real slice of the action. No more fees. Fees!" She sniffed. "That's just..."

"Dill pickles." I said.

"Yeah honey. Just dill pickles."

"So what's the law changing that needs to be done?"

"We'll get to that in good time. So are you in?"

"As in as I can be." I said. Here was I about to promote a man I couldn't vote for and now I was sitting in a the world's most expensive pick-up truck making tentative promises about land deals that I already knew were worth billions.

She stayed leaning close to me. I'm certain she licked her lips but maybe it was just a thought.

"One thing, honey. Only one thing you gotta do for me."

I breathed in the intoxicating milieu. "What's that?"

Her voice was breathless. "You gotta get rid of that British person, the little effeminate on your payroll. And take all the electronic files and give them back to me. Give it to me. All the files."

"And what if the answer is no?"

She paused. She was still close. Outside it was fully dark and another car passed as the birds settled in the hissing gums. It was time to move.

"Is the answer no?" She said. It was breathless and it wasn't Sunday School or the Perpetual Sisters of Mercy breathlessness.

"My answer is, Robert is going nowhere but we finish making your husband PM? You OK about that?"

She pulled back and the window whirred down. She raised an arm and beckoned Brother Underwood from the darkness.

"I am definitely not OK about that. But, a deal is a deal. You stay on the PM project. It's too late to jump ship for either side. You got all those polls and focus group results and the preselection meeting is next week Sure, you finish that, but on the Big Plan thing, honey, you are O-U-T out and you're gonna live to regret that. The chance of a lifetime and everybody around here would have been happy. Now we got a problem. A big, big problem that we gotta resolve."

"Resolve?"

She patted my knee briskly and leant forward, eyes fixed. "Your Robbity Bob Malahide is still the problem. He's been spying on us."

"Spying's a bit harsh"

"OK. Have it your own way. Let's just say he's a big nose. And people with big noses usually get them shortened and, honey, nobody ever knows who did the surgery. Fact of life." She said and shook her head as if it was a painful eternal truth.

SIXTEEN

Through a glass darkly

The Tasmanian Highlands are a fisherman's dream if you glorify standing in waders up to your thighs trying to outsmart a trout and failing. For two centuries, cattlemen and sheep herders lived in their split timber and stone chimney cottages, moving the animals backwards and forwards to take advantage of greener pastures each season. Before then, the aboriginal tribes migrated each year from the coast, firing the bush on the way to make better hunting grounds. That pattern didn't last long when the British Empire decided that every second son or respectable settler was entitled to shoo away the dark tribes with a judicious mixture of legal and physical strategies. Now, only the alpine ghost gums and myrtles at dusk hint at their forty thousand year presence.

"Nope, Paddy. I'm telling you nothing unless you get off your arse and come fishing with me or surfing at dusk at Carlton beach. Your choice." Charles Wooley said.

"C'mon mate. Just a few words. Who else but you would be polyglot enough to know anything about trusts and South Dakota?"

"Reception's breaking up. Never very good up here in the Highlands." He said.

"OK, OK. What's the deal?"

"Told you. Look Paddy, I'm a lonely old man and I need company when I surf..."

"At dusk for Chrissake, that's when the sharks feed..."

"Or when I trout fish."

"Yeah and the Highlands are crawling with snakes."

There was a pause on the phone and I could hear the wind blowing across the button grass.

"Charlie, it's a long way to travel just to hear something you can tell me on the phone. I haven't even got a fishing licence"

"Reception's bad...falling out!" The line went dead.

Time was ticking before the Liberal Party pre-selections. I was trying to think of anyone else who could possibly know about South Dakota trust funds and I was already down to a list of my shadier acquaintances who lived in shadier places than Tasmania, when Charles rang back.

"I've just paid for a licence. Cost me twenty three bucks so don't pike out. I've got enough spare gear for you. I'll meet you at Bronte. Should only take a couple of hours for you to get there." He said.

Bronte Park is one of the early Hydro Electric Commission villages built for the workers and their families who built the power schemes that built the heavy industry like paper mills, zinc works and aluminum smelters that came to run Tasmanian politics in a cozy alliance of unions, bosses and politicians. Although, nowadays, they are only a few skeletons just holding on while a new breed of tourist developers, casinos and fisheries steal the political clout that makes governments wary.

I took my time driving up the Lyle Highway through towns like Hamilton and Ouse, old sandstone nineteenth century towns deep in Glover-like rolling dry pasture lands until you hit the high country which always feels like it's waited all year for the snow to cover the button grass and winds to blast the stunted alpine gums. I stopped once for coffee in Hamilton where I selected pastries and analysed home-made jams and I stopped again to watch a wombat nibble on the roadside. Then there was the echidna hiding in full sight like a child at a birthday party. Finally, when I could no longer delay the act of trout persecution I drove the mountainous highway to Bronte.

Just past the General Store Charles was waiting near the house he and his Scottish born parents once lived in during the Hydro schemes' glory days when half the world turned up in Tassie to escape Russians or make a few dollars or a new life, whichever was easier. His four wheel drive carried the dust of ten thousand years. Being a television hot-shot meant he could surf and fish in between writing a weekly article for the local *Mercury* and reporting from hot spots like Kabul. *"Always compliment the chef in Kabul, he could be Taliban."* Today I was pushing the deadline of Tommy's pre-selection and I was looking for more wisdom than that, although we had readily exchanged what we called *thankfully forgotten wisdom* since our days at University together.

I took a good look at his 4WD. "Still saving the planet?" I said.

He ran his eye over my Mercedes. "Still exploiting the South African workers?"

"It's German." I said.

"It's made in South Africa." He said. We had that type of relationship.

"I'm here now, so tell me about South Dakota."

He smiled and held out a pair of rubber waders and a fishing rod at me like he was offering the holy sacrament. "It's the home of Mount Rushmore where they have the gigantic heads of Presidents. Trump's next in line"

"Yep. Got that. Trusts in South Dakota. I know it rings a bell with you so c'mon, deliver."

He smiled again and assumed a sphinx like air. "Not so fast Paddy boy, we've got some fishing to do. It's for your own health and well-being you know. Ah, the peace, the emotions recollected in tranquility. You will one day thank me for this."

We walked across the button grass plains with the stream curving and meandering, neat as a chateau garden until it reached some low hanging trees where trout hold themselves against the flow, daring us to get closer. A movement in the button grass attracted my sensitised eyes. A black Tiger snake flowed like molten glass into the tussock taking a pulse or two of my heart beat with it.

"Charles. There's a snake."

"Yes."

"I mean. This is exactly what I said about coming to these types of places."

He turned and lifted his hand, beckoning me to walk more quietly. He crouched and moved forward, eyes on the stream.

"Snake." I whispered as another showed only its tail as it lazily disappeared.

"Could be a griffin or a basilisk." He whispered.

I fiddled with my rod and reel displaying a highly developed sense of clumsiness for which the trout must have been grateful. The flies were already tied for me so I stepped into the enervating water after some brutal instructions from Charles about the care of fish and the respect that salmonids deserve from people like us and how fly fishers don't talk and what was the smallest trout I could bully and why the trout can only be seen by a subtle change in the water surface. It was heart stopping stuff that, once Charles finally got around to telling me about the trust funds of South Dakota, I would readily forget.

I kept up the pretense of communicating with trout for a couple of long hours. I figured they hated me as much as I hated them so we were all square by five o'clock when Charles decided it was time for lunch. Lunch at five in the afternoon had to be some sort of Isle of Arran joke or maybe he was trying to recoup the twenty three bucks he'd paid for my licence.

He opened his basket and lifted a brown trout in respectful hands. He lowered it gently into the stream and we watched it dart away, its spots and fin soon only a slight whirl on the waters.

"A beauty." He said and didn't bother asking if I'd caught anything.

We sat on the wet grass and ate rye bread sand-witches. The coffee from the thermos tasted better as the afternoon sun quietly withdrew and the temperature started to drop. A hawk hovered on the slip stream and other life stayed still in the button grass. Charles emptied his plastic cup and poured another.

"So, South Dakota. There's got to be a song in it. *I left my heart in Sioux Falls*. Doesn't have the same ring to it." He said.

I took another coffee. It smelt better than the whole of Colombia "So, why would entrepreneurs want to put their money into special trust funds in South Dakota?"

He shrugged. "Because South Dakota is the gold medalist of the trust fund world."

"The rich can pick anywhere to hide their money. The Cayman Islands, Switzerland, anywhere." I said.

"Ah. The Caymans and Switzerland *used* to be the place to hide it, out of the reach of the tax man. But, these days, the Swiss have to kiss the backside of the European Union. And a lot of other tax havens that hide the big money aren't too politically stable. If you are salting it away for the long term you need a stable government that is going to change the rules to look after your money no matter what happens anywhere else in the world. Look, you're going to have to tell me a little more. Why are you asking?"

The afternoon sun had almost completely gone and it was ghost time in that isolated place. So many had passed this way for thousands of years. Barefoot and greased, horses pulling ploughs and excavating equipment, shepherds in their lonely huts curled up as the howling winds or snow went deeper into the night. Lot of time and space moving around in history.

"Let's say that someone was investing and making big money and it's all being hidden in trust funds in South Dakota." I said.

He looked at me, waiting for further explanations.

"And?"

"And, it will run into billions."

"Do they have families that they want to protect forever? Like great, great, grandkids?"

I thought about what Tammy Rayfinger said last night about her kids and heritage.

"I guess so."

"Well the purpose of trust funds is to keep the money secret and make sure it stays in the family forever. It's what the rich like to do. So let's get back to South Dakota. Back in the 1980s the state was almost broke and this Governor, what a ripper he was, thought he and Citibank could do a deal so he changed all the banking laws. Overnight. Changed the credit card interest rate so they could charge what they liked. It all went from there. They then altered their trust laws with the same alacrity. Even making sure that creditors couldn't get at the money to recover debts."

"Just overnight?"

"Alacrity means overnight. They can do it that way because they have a legislature that does what the Governator wants. They keep changing the laws to hide the dough, escape tax and stay ahead of the other tax escape countries or the other US states like Delaware. But, the big mother of them all, is their abolition of the perpetual trust restrictions. You know what a perpetual trust is?"

"It's like catching trout."

"Lackaday Paddy, not in your case. Well, most trusts in the world expire after one hundred years. Not in South Dakota. They abolished the oldest most valuable controls over trusts, abolished the long standing rule against perpetuities. In South Dakota a trust can now go on forever, stay in the family, like incest."

I thought about all the rich families in the world who would be out there shopping around for compliant governments that could help you keep the family money for ever, ignore creditors with impunity, pay no taxes and be eternal, financially that is. Probably even set up trusts for their pooches. If Team Tommy and Tammy were sending it all to South Dakota, the only thing standing in their way was the Day of Judgement coming earlier than expected.

"He took a gun to a hostage scene and got blown off the road by a tornado." Charles said.

"Who did?"

"Governor Wild Bill Janklow. He was ex-Marines. Got a little excitable sometimes."

Then we fished some more in the dusk and Charles told me about the ephemeroptera or mayflies or red spinners as some call them on which many fishing flies are based, how they struggle to get a life, to make it to adulthood and then get eaten by trout, birds and so on but some species had two penises and how they last just twenty four hours as adults and they are not around some rivers now because they have been affected by pollutants. It was riveting in its way because I kept making some kind of connection between ephemeroptera, *Coming Now* and Patrick Kennedy and Associates.

Back in the shack that night we listened to the wind as the fire crackled and I started to relax which wasn't easy when you keep thinking about clients that had taken over everyone's lives and were looking to do the same for the whole country. Charles seemed pretty relaxed too. I knew this because he kept humming one of the great tuneless operas and was scrupulously egg and bread crumbing the day's catch then placing the trout carefully into medium heated oil. *Medium heat. Gutted immediately after catching. Boned from an incision across the tail. Serve with a good Tasmanian Pinot Gris or dry Riesling.*

The key of knowledge

"Haven't you finished yet?" I said. I was getting edgy. Working for a client you despised didn't help the atmosphere around the place.

Helen and Robert were hunched over their screens as they played and replayed the proposed promo for Pastor Tommy's pre-selection presentation. We figured that the pre-selection panel would be impressed with a full blown version that was already campaign and TV ready. Later this version would be run big time on all TV stations bar the ABC. Other versions would be sliced and diced and distributed via TV and social media but there would be thousands of slightly different versions that would be targeted directly at individuals all around the Lyons electorate, depending on their occupations, political prejudices, environmental preferences, family circumstances and whether or not they like cats and dogs or pet crocodiles or whatever special hobbies and obsessions that Big Friend collected about them. That way, everyone got to have a special video on Facebook, Instagram and WhatsApp, just for themselves. That's the kind of friendly service that Patrick Kennedy and Associates were providing to make Australia a better place.

"Got the spectrum right." Helen said and hit the button to pause the video. On the TV screen, the start of the cricket season was conveniently timed to allow Clive Palmer's yellow badged adverts to bash the Labor Party and its trendy mates who wanted to kill the coal industry, Australia's weekends and make pensioners very afraid.

Clive appears in a white shirt and tie and trousers straining and was letting us know that Labor Leader Bill Shorten was shifty, couldn't lie straight in bed. Clive was going to fix that and make Australia Great Again. Then the cricket came on again and Australians were back in the deep sleep.

"Robert. Are you with us?" I said.

Robert shook his head. "Remarkable."

"Yeah, spending all that money to influence an election." I said.

"No. Gary Lyon. He can put the ball on a ten cent piece. I love it when he takes on left handed batsmen."

Helen looked across at Clive Palmers large frame filling the screen. "$60 million goes a long way."

"How much?"

She looked at me as if I'd just holidayed on Mars. "Yeah. Sixty million. That's what Clive Palmer is spending on anti-Labor adverts."

I had seen some of the adverts and they looked pretty hand-made but if you spend that much, there'll be enough takers to make it worth your while. *They're not taking my weekends or 4WD's.* You knew what PM Scott Morrison was going to do with that material as the phony election started to warm up. Scott Morrison was going to win because a former Labor PM said he couldn't see where Labor was going to win the necessary extra seats. But, we weren't interested in that election. We and *Coming Now* had our sights firmly on the next because we knew that, one election over, they would be pre-selecting candidates for the next. All sitting members would be preselected but the others were going to be done as soon as possible after Scott Morrison took his wife and kids on stage and claimed a miracle and divine intervention.

"Clive Palmer, you'd better watch out. You better not shout.

Coming Now is coming to town." I said.

"You really mean that don't you?" Helen said.

"Yeah. I reckon. *Coming Now* will outspend Clive Palmer next time round."

"You really do mean it." Helen said and pressed *go* to run the Pastor Tommy promo and we settle back to watch Tommy and Tammy and Debbie and Ruthie walking through Lucerne paddocks like a clip from the Sound of Music. That dissolved to a clip of Tommy and Tammy leaning on the fence of a sheep yard, moleskins and checked shirt but no hats. More shots of Tammy and Tommy in a supermarket contained the deathless phrase from Tammy. *In difficult times we know that every household is stretched and we have to tighten our belts.* Grateful pensioners got a run as well as the usual happy sporty healthy kids who loved their Weetbix and didn't mind making their own vegemite sandwiches for school lunches, which in itself was a miracle that Tommy would bring to every household.

Helen turned round and put her sneakers on the desk which was ok with me since I had sworn I would never interfere with the computer den that she and Robert had somehow made a home. The whiteboard was full of key phrases and a list of video story- boards.

"Where's the football?" I said.

Robert said. "I cut it out. You know, not everybody actually follows football."

I said. "You're correct."

"Thank you." Robert said and was about to work on the titles.

"Not everyone follows football. I know one at least who doesn't follow football. He's a bloke who's been living up a tree, making a protest about forests. But there are four million people who watched AFL last year"

"Seven and a half million who attend games" Helen said.

"Yeah. A lot. Maybe some of them may be footy followers. Please put the footy back in."

Helen's flicking hands told the story but, just to rub it in, she tapped and brought up a montage of Tommy's great days on the arena. Tommy making desperate last minute lunges, clever side steps and an accurate pass, a number of spectacular marks and shots of the crowd applauding and roaring. I nodded approval but then a title appeared to the sound of Wagner's Ride of the Walkyries. It said *written and authorised by Paddy Kennedy, football failure and tragic.*

"Very funny."

"We've got one week before the pre-selection panel meets." Helen said, beating me to it. I hate it when co-workers predict your nagging.

"Correct." I said.

"Exactly correct." She said.

"You two spend too much time in front of the screen." I said.

"Too much time putting lipstick on pigs." Helen said to my departing back. Robert avoided my eyes which I took to be agreement.

When I went into the reception area, Donna looked confused. She quickly moved a magazine out of my sight but her flushed face gave the game away. In the Huon Valley they don't do subterfuge well.

"What's that?" I said.

Donna kept her hand firmly on the magazine but it didn't take Dinny Dinham's experience to know that Donna was reading the story which proclaimed, LOVE AND INTELLIGENCE BEGINS IN THE WOMB.

"Hope or reality?" I said and the confusion went into overdrive.

"It's too early." Donna mumbled to her desk, very out of sorts, with slightly puffy skin compared with her usual apple blossom freshness.

"Yeah. You're only twenty."

"Too early to tell, Mr. Kennedy. You know."

"You mean."

"Yes. I mean..." She looked quickly at her belly then recovered.

"Like?"

"You know."

"Well that's cleared that one up." I said, remembering some of the advice HR Kathy had given me when we had an HR person. *Never make personal comments to staff.*

On the radio, the media were still praising the electoral miracle that had put Liberal PM Scott Morrison back into office. Morrison was especially thanking Queenslanders and Tasmanians for getting him over the line. All the other political parties went into hiding like autumn leaves blown away except Clive Palmer who claimed victory for the Liberals although his name changing party actually didn't win any seats. It was the end of summer and a lot of other things as well.

I had the list of the pre-selection panel and was working through any other contacts I could remotely use to win them over when Robert knocked on the door. He had his lap-top with him.

"The football's back in." He said.

"Is that an apology?" I said.

He shrugged. When push came to shove, Robert gave no ground but he never complained if his advice was ignored.

"The promo looks quite good now, actually. I clipped the football so that anyone could see that Reverend Rayfinger was a brilliant athlete."

"Pastor."

"Pardon?"

"He's Pastor not Reverend."

"Hmm." Robert said and I knew what he meant.

"So everything's in place for next weekend's pre-selection?"

"Absolutely. But, there *is* something I need to show you." Robert said and opened his laptop. He ran an aerial video which soon became apparent was of the *Coming Now* headquarters. From that height you could grasp how enormous the campus was. Hangars, school, playing fields, exercise yards and obstacle courses all marching away from the administration building and the church with its hints of a mosque despite the large cross dominating the skyline. There were kids obviously competing in a cross country event as they climbed the hills. Some distance away, Lilliputian figures of stragglers emerged from bushland and the hawthorn hedges that dissected the rolling untended hills. You could also see a security fence as it skirted the hundreds of hectares west of the buildings. When Dinny said the Rayfingers were into real estate he was spot on.

"Thanks to Dr. Google." I said.

Robert shook his head and rolled his eyes. "That's not Google. That's our live feed from one of *Coming Now's* drones. They don't know we've captured it and that we can watch whenever they do anything." He seemed quite pleased with that. I was quite pleased with that. The spies spy on the spies again. It suggested a close and intimate relationship.

"Cross country?" I suggested.

"Hmm. You'd think so but with a difference. Now let's zoom in on these kiddy pops." He manipulated the camera so that it zoomed in on a group who were sitting at camp tables at the end of the course. All the runners sooner or later came to the tables and registered the completion of their run.

"And?"

"See them look at their watches and fiddle with them and point them at the laptops on the tables?"

"Yes. Recording their times." I said. "Apparently, half the country times their physical steps or runs or heartbeats on those things. So what?"

Helen stood in the doorway. "Actually all those little activity and health apps like Strava, Runkeeper, Googlefit, MapMyRun, have over three hundred million users. Big data base, lots of lovely details about people's lives and it's all very competitive and the data can be sold to cities to help planning and traffic flows. One of them even knows what day of the week is the most popular for people to exercise, city by city. Pretty cool."

"Very invasive and addictive." Robert said. "Someone is controlling your life. Like a God."

"Yeah. That too." said Helen.

Helen and Robert. Their backgrounds were so very different but you could detect that both had clambered their way up unique ladders of their own that led to their own private worlds. From time to time, special people would be permitted entrée but the rules were subject to changes more complex than a mobile phone contract. Still a lot of people work with people they hate or just tolerate so we were doing ok.

"Want to take a drive?" I said.

The traffic was light even if Tasmanians always complained about it so we arrived at the *Coming Now* compound as the cross country event was winding down. We avoided the administration block and the drone hangar and walked quickly to the camp tables. The kids were mainly teenagers, some spotty but most were gangly pure skinned kids that ate their vegetables even if some of them had to work at McDonalds to pay their tithes.

They were mostly breathless and excited and few paid us any attention or if they did, it was done obliquely as if adults allowed into the compound were figures who automatically commanded respect and authority. All crowded around the laptops of the recorders who downloaded the wrist devices and punched code into a computer. The same drone that Robert had tracked was still hovering discreetly overhead.

Helen said. "Really disciplined kids. Those bloody health watch devices! They banned them in Afghanistan because they gave positional information away; the enemy knew where our guys were because our guys were the only ones exercising in that area. Jeez. No wonder we lost people."

Robert sniffed. Young people could have been from Kazakhstan for all he cared. But he was closely watching the procedure as the panting red faced runners uploaded the data into the laptops. It was an orderly, obviously familiar process.

For a religious group they were dressed as any other teenagers, tentatively stretching the propriety rules that would have disallowed tight shorts and T-shirts and artificially tanned legs. I had noticed that at all their events run by *Coming Now*. It was a discreet *let kids be fashionable* dress code.

"So good. Awesome. Seventy on one hundred, pinged it. Rianna. You are so awesome."

"What are we doing here with these kiddy pops?" Helen said. This was her old milieu, meaning that ten kilometres before breakfast would be another way to meet the desert sun-rise. Anyone who ran for fun had to have rocks in their heads. I was looking at her red hair and elegant sharp features in the afternoon sun with the hills behind and the chattering and gossiping of the kids when I spotted Jacinta the young girl from the Mall in Hobart.

"Look and learn." I said and headed in the young girl's direction.

"Hello Mr…" Jacinta said, looking up from her table.

"Kennedy."

"Yes. Mr. Kennedy. Dianna, you've not registered. Hold it closer to the laptop. Great! Thank you." she said. Her voice had that upwards intonation at the end of a sentence that has taken two hundred years to evolve.

"Pretty cool gear." I said.

"Oh so cool." Jacinta said.

"It must be able to collect a lot of data."

"Testing. We're testing the health data first then tomorrow we're doing a demonstration of the drones." She said. Her face had that perfection that teen magazine's would kill for. Perfect teeth, clear skin and blonde hair that was still shiny. And the purple painted fingernails had survived the shifts at McDonalds.

"The drones. Yes. They are great." I said.

She looked pleased. "We're going to do a demonstration of how our drones can deliver fast food, newspapers and coffee to people at Salamanca Markets. You can order a cup of coffee and it gets delivered by our drones. We've got twenty of them ready to go on Saturday week. We call it *Coming Now, Delivery Now*. That's part of our *Jobmaker* project It's so rad."

"It's definitely rad." I said. "And what are you testing here today with this health thing?"

"We're testing the capacity of the system."

"What, to learn how much you can upload in seconds before it crashes?"

She looked at me sweetly. "Sort of. Except, it doesn't crash. Everything we collect today will be in Big Friend and analysed for patterns and sorted into each person's health and running file...within oh, within five seconds. Then we have a daily history of everybody who want to be healthy.We're doing the mathematics on it. Exponential growth. And we figure that, within six months there'll be millions using it because it will be a free app. Cool."

"Hyper cool." I said expertly.

Well, it *was* hyper-cool until Helen said *uh, oh* and I said, *problem* as a black Volkswagen Amorak bounced and thumped its way across the paddock. Its lights were on even though it wasn't dusk. It pulled up in front of Helen and me and, before it was fully stationary, the passenger door opened and Lieutenant Squeaky (Army Reserve) leaped out. It wasn't elegant but he was pretty quick on his feet. He carried a mobile phone in his hands although it was obvious he already knew who we were.

"Nice drone." I said.

He placed his mobile into a shirt sleeve pocket that once upon a time, trendies used to carry their cigarettes. He didn't look up at the drone which was now hovering directly above us. He pointed at Helen and Robert in turn. "We must have missed you at reception." His voice was as flat and as neutral as a pancake.

"Yep, rang the bell. Nobody there." I said.

"We don't have a bell." He said.

"Buzzer?"

He ignored me and beckoned to young Jacinta before walking away from us. She followed meekly and we could see the body language go crazy as he stood over her then almost turned his back on her as she tried to explain. He half listened to her and then got back on his mobile. She tried to approach him but he waved her away. She headed our way, collected her laptop and phone and almost ran in the direction of the administration block. The tears in her eyes told the whole story and more about Coming Now modus operandi.

Helen turned to see her go then pivoted on me, "How long do we have to work for these bastards?" she said and started to walk back to our car.

Robert had detached himself and was waiting to hear my response. I used to think that Robert wanted to avoid conflict but I had gradually come to accept that he had an inner core that could have been bottled and sold to gymnasiums.

"So?" he asked.

"So... what?"

"How long before we can flick them?" He looked somewhere east of Eden and put both hands in his pockets. But before he could whistle a tune Lieutenant Squeaky was standing directly in front of me. He had eyes that would have helped Van Gogh sell his first and only painting. Eyes give the game away, always, except, with this young tyro who had perfected the art of avoidance by deliberately looking straight through you.

"I thought Robert had pressed the bell and he thought I had. Sorry. It gets like that when we're busy." I said. Squeaky made absolutely no comment but continued his title fight with my eyes.

Robert was used to the behaviour of lions and buffaloes so dealing with Squeaky was a push-over. I would have throttled Squeaky with his own thin black tie and gagged him with that clean short sleeved shirt but Robert was made of sterner stuff. "Yes, the bell. We've been very busy finishing the preselection video before next week-end. Comes up very well, very well indeed."

We stood there while the teenagers loaded and uploaded then did what kids do, boys pushing each other while the girls stood pigeon toed and whispered then laughed self-consciously, out of sync with what was really going on.

"When do we get it?" Squeaky said and licked his lips as if having dry lips was a weakness. It was a precise movement that he'd probably practiced in a mirror. Momentarily, I imagined that he also secretly bought body building equipment from carefully hidden magazines but the thin arms killed that idea.

Robert looked at me.

"Tomorrow." I said.

"Good." Squeaky said and started to walk to the pick-up truck without another word or gesture. I noticed that *Coming Soon* was obeying the golden rule of never taking off-road vehicles actually off road. I also managed to catch the still life image of Brother

Underwood as he sat immobile in the driver's seat. In the distance, autumn storm clouds were building over the rounded bare hills. It was country that made you uncomfortable, as if too many people, either unshod or booted, had walked across its slopes too many times and had failed to leave a trace.

"We'd better get back mate," I said to Robert. "There's storm coming and we don't want to be out there like Hamlet."

"King Lear."

"What?"

"King Lear was the one who was caught out in the storm, with his Fool."

It wasn't a day to debate Shakespeare. I was determined to make some tough decisions but the timing had to be right and the last place to make decisions was out there in that virtual prison waiting for the wind to sweep in the rains. One thing I did know then was fools and kings make mistakes like associating with dangerous weirdoes.

"Out damn spot." I said to no-one in particular as the rain swept in and the kids ran knock kneed squealing, trying to avoid puddles or step in them, depending on their character or urgings. For some inexplicable reason, Robert and I stood in the rain, allowing the drops to spot our jackets then seep into our shirts and suits like a cleansing moment that wouldn't come again.

EIGHTEEN

The sting of death

When I arrived the police cars and ambulance were there, blue and red lights flashing on the faces of cops and ambos. A few neighbours in dressing gowns or track suits were being interviewed or were pretending they were about to be interviewed. The Sergeant who'd been with Dinny a few weeks ago was quick to see me and seek me out. Helen stood quietly beside as the young cop laboriously took my name and address and relationship to the deceased. She kept referring to Robert as the deceased as if she was rehearsing for a court appearance. Dinny saw us and was at her side muttering a few words that meant nick off.

"I'll take care of this."

He looked exhausted and wary.

"Why?" I said.

"You two are not bloody supposed to be here. This is a potential crime scene and I've got all these gawkers and reporters tramping all over the place." He looked at the young cop who was filling her note book fast enough.

"Look. He was your workmate. It's gonna be hard and I sympathise. Right now, it looks like suicide. OK? But between you and me, I'm leaving the door open. So I don't want you around. He's been identified." He let that sink in.

"By who?" Helen said. There were no tears just a fixed face changing colours in time with the cop cars and ambulance. Her croaky voice was the only give-away.

"Neighbours. They're certain." He indicated the young Sergeant. "She also did an ID. She remembers him from the last time you were here."

The Sergeant had climbed into one of the cop cars and was using the radio. Disembodied voices and crackling echoed in the streets around. House lights were on until their occupants obviously lost interest or rubbernecked from the safety of their darkened windows.

"How did it happen?" I said. There was a chill in the dark that had nothing to do with the weather.

"Can't say. Balcony. That's all I can tell you now. It's a big fall onto concrete. No signs of a struggle or forced entry. Nothing."

"Can we see him?" Helen said so quietly Dinny at first didn't hear her.

"No. I told you it's a potential crime scene. I'm bloody sorry. I know what you two thought about Pommie Bob...the deceased. But, I have to do this by the book. I'll take a statement later but for now, I gotta ask you Paddy, where were you between eleven last night and now?"

"I was at home. All night."

"And you, Mrs Troy."

Helen hesitated. She cleared her throat. "I was with him. With Mr.Kennedy. All night. It's Ms."

"Sorry?"

"It's Ms. It's Ms.Troy. If this is a formal record, you...uh...need to know." She said gratuitously.

Dinny's face was impassive. He had never made any reference to the relationship between Helen and me. He took out a Spirex notebook that had seen better days and laboriously wrote down our responses. He flipped the note book shut and placed it inside his suit.

"Well, that's all for now. I will need to talk to you tomorrow, after I do the...uh...forensics. I've got a good sheila on that. She won't leave any stone unturned."

He stood awkwardly as paramedics closed the ambulance door. There was a pause then suddenly the flashing lights stopped as it pulled away quietly into the night. Dinny was looking for words that didn't cross the line.

"I'm sorry about your loss." He was still fixed to the spot, the remaining cop car's lights flashing red and blue at his beefy face. Then he shook his head almost fiercely. "I liked Pommie Bob. He was a good man."

We met at the usual spot along Sandy Bay Beach except this time it was different. Dinny wore a suit and sombre tie and Helen was with me. The three of us sat on the bench. The young cop was nowhere to be seen unless she was amongst some of the early morning swimmers and joggers who were busy extending their lives. I felt a pang of resentment.

"It still looks like no suspicious circumstances. Blood alcohol reading very high. No signs of a struggle, an accident. That's all we know. It's just a bloody dead end." Dinny said flatly.

"And Simeon Brady?" Helen said.

"Who's Simeon Brady?" I asked.

"That freak who was sending me the phone messages. From Afghanistan." She said evenly. It was the first time I had heard her mention his name but, with Helen, some things just stayed buried then got released when the time was right. Just asking never worked.

Dinny snorted then remembered himself. He noticed my confused look.

"You know about this Simeon Brady?" he said to me. I nodded.

"Right, he's off the list of suspects. I can tell you this officially because it's to do with another separate case. He's a fucking loony and we'll get him on the misuse of a carriage service to harass and threaten." He turned to me, "That's using the phone system to..."

"I know what it is. Why is he off the list of suspects?"

"Because he's in the US of A, at a fucking gun show, would you believe? Well, the AFP in Australia and the Yanks are both gonna clobber him about those abusive calls. They got him on toast thanks to you. But I wanna know if he makes any contact with you. If he does, he's gonna get a little visit to have big one way talkies. You understand?"

I looked at Helen closely. She smiled, a creaky disappointed smile like that issue was the least of her concerns.

For a while each of us sat immersed in our own thoughts as the waves hissed and withdrew. Now and then one would thump, out of sync with the others. Helen was over thugs like Simeon Brady and she'd done it on her own. Normally, that would have cause for celebration but Robert's lonely death couldn't be turned around that easily.

Helen reached in her back-pack and pulled out a few pages of copied emails which she gave to Dinny. Dinny took a while to read them.

"What a bunch of pricks!" He puffed his cheeks in disbelief and handed them to me.

"Who's *polo@comingnow.com.au*?" I said.

Helen looked at me with disbelief. "It's that one you call Squeaky. Marcus Gormley, Marcus, Marco. Marco Polo. Polo. Get it?"

I looked closely at the respondent's email. Squeaky was clearly close to another person with the email moniker of *taker*. Helen lifted her face. Her reply was dull as if the life and energy had gone from her.

"Taker, as in Underwood, undertaker. These boys are very predictable. I found this on Robert's other computer this morning. The one that you asked him to take off the internet."

I read the emails. There was a lot of discussion between Squeaky and Underwood about deep fakes and the potential to take an opponent's image and edit in new words that would embarrass them. One suggestion from Lieutenant Squeaky recommended that rape jokes and racist rubbish could be put into the mouths of the unfortunate opponent then circulated on the internet.

"Nice." I said.

"Take a look at the next lot," Dinny said.

One from Squeaky assessed the potential threat that Kennedy and Associates could pose if we fell out with *Coming Now* or the Project as he called it.

Squeaky: *Big potential problem. How to deal with it?*

The response from Underwood was brief and to the point. *If Kennedy splits with the Project, load their systems with bad child porn and call the cops. Stage one.*

Squeaky: *What is stage two?*

Underwood: *You take a guess.*

Dinny was still shaking his head in disbelief.

"I've seen this type of set up before. Kids do it in juvenile detention if they can't get what they want from the warders or social workers. Same in the big boys' jail. Stuff someone's reputation for a packet of cigarettes but I have never seen this kind of thing before with these kind of people...these blokes are Christians!" He exploded. A runner in those skimpy shorts that show your buttocks paused and jogged on the spot, looking back.

"Everything OK?" he said.

"Piss off mate," Dinny said and tapped the paper in my hand. "Listen. This doesn't prove that somebody killed Pommie Bob...your mate. We can pass it on to the AFP and they'll deal with it under the..."

"Misuse of a carriage service." I said.

"Yep. Just say the word. But, it's a long way from planting child porn on someone to actual murder. A long way." Dinny said. You could tell from his slumped figure that he had reached a dead end.

"I'll gather the rest of the files. They'll be with you this afternoon." Helen said.

"Good." Said Dinny and said *bloody Christians* again.

"OK. We'll gather and cache the lot but...they are going nowhere. Not to Dinny not to anybody" I said. I looked at their astonished faces. Helen snorted in disgust.

"Patrick. Robert is dead. Probably murdered. You can't just collect the evidence and leave it at that. That is just bloody gutless!"

"Helen. Just collect the evidence, time stamp it and do not use a networked computer with access to the internet. Please." I went to touch her shoulder but she pulled away, her face red and angry

Dinny leaned forward, letting his hands hang loosely between his legs. You could hear the cogs go round in his head. Then, with head still lowered, he turned to stare at me. I could see the redness of his eyes. "You're up to something aren't you?"

The good samaritan

Robert's funeral was held in a small church and I was soon to discover why. When we arrived, his coffin was already on a gurney covered with an Australian flag except that the Union Jack part of the flag faced the congregation. There were lilies and roses strewn on the thin carpet around the coffin and one of Robert's wild life photographs was amongst the flowers.

The little church was full to overflowing and there were more people crowding round the simple wooden doors. They were what the upper class would have called a motley crew. Some did look as if they would be searching for a home later that evening. Amongst the faded cardigans and missing teeth were a smattering of smartly dressed fashionistas, buzz cuts and strategically dyed hair; the two worlds of Robert Malahide.

The professionally po-faced attendants ushered Helen and me to the front.

"Relatives." The attendant said, cleared his throat and pointed to the front row which was empty. We sat and tried to avoid looking at the coffin of the man who, a short time ago, was family. I started thinking about the things I had said to Robert and the things that had been left unsaid, like praise. Then there was unexplained anger which welled up inside me, like a blocked drain, poisoning the moment.

The organist began playing Bach and Schubert and it was calming to just absorb the centuries and continuity behind the music. I pressed Helen's hand but she didn't respond, just stared straight ahead. We had barely spoken since yesterday when I called a halt to the doomed investigation of *Coming Now*'s possible involvement in Robert's death. There was a lot to talk about but I was not going to move until I knew what pieces we had on the board. Until then, I was thinking about nothing else but how we could honour Robert in a way that he would have approved.

There was a shuffle and Dinny slid into our pew. He was breathless and uncomfortable in that place. He nodded self-consciously. Out of the corner of my eye I surveyed the mourners. They were a queer mix of younger people in badly knotted collar and ties alongside others who looked as if they couldn't have afforded either.

The music stopped and a young priest came to the steps, clothed from top to bottom in heavy black. He had strange angular features as if someone had banged his head on both sides with two heavy Bibles. I noticed his long thin hands were clean and white like a chemist. He held them in a gesture of prayer while two other acolytes in black stood imitating his stance while another held the incense. *Three black crows with pink faces.*

"Dearly beloved. I am Father Copeman. We are gathered here to repose the soul of our brother Robert Francis de Lacey Malahide."

"Didn't know he had a handle like that?" Dinny muttered to himself. The full name was another surprise but there was more to come.

I try to avoid funerals or hospitals, seeing that they're full of dead or sick people. At the couple of funerals I'd been to there'd been an informal ceremony that allowed the mourners to dredge up a few personal anecdotes, maybe even a laugh or two, a slide show, a bit of recorded music while the priest tried to pronounce the deceased's name correctly. This time it was different from the word go.

Father Copeman cleared his throat again. It was a voice that belonged in an empty tomb.

"Robert's parents cannot be here today but they have expressly requested that Robert's mass be celebrated in the...uh...traditional form."

Father Copeman made a formalistic but wry apology to Pope John the Twenty Third which went entirely over the heads of most of the congregation. Then the service proceeded in Latin with incense, the ringing of bells and three acolytes giving it the works. I looked at Dinny who recognised the extraordinary ceremony with a shrug of his shoulders? I'd never asked but I always assumed Dinny was a nominal Catholic in the grand old Tassie police game of Masons versus Catholics. It didn't require Dinny's copper's instinct to know that this service was probably without Robert's approval. Helen and half the congregation sat like onlookers as the ancient responses were recited by the few old-timer parishioners still familiar with the words. A handful of modern believers responded with their Amens. That clashed with the Des Iraes of the old-timers like double booked concerts. In a strange way, it was comforting to know that the whole service was impersonal, an *insert the deceased's name here* type of formal liturgy that didn't keep reminding us of Robert the real person lying there in that coffin.

"Requiem aeternam dona eis Domine."

The service droned on robotically. Robert's funeral service without Robert. There was a lot of the old liturgy about man being inherently evil and the inevitable horror of the afterlife in hell. Each little sin was a wound in the body of Christ which was nothing compared with the murder of unborn infants and so on. Finally, the listing of punishment and sins ran out of steam, the priest elongating the words of the final punishment like the echoes of a haunted house. He stepped back, hands together to watch his handiwork. All he got was more shuffling and a few coughs as buttocks moved to get some circulation back.

Then, a young guy in a fashionably thin suit and a stubble beard stepped forward. The shuffling stopped. Without an announcement, he broke into a high countertenor rendition of an Elizabethan song. From the first bar, you knew in that little church that hearts were beating stronger and breath was taken away by the purity of the voice.

"What is love? Tis gone before
The morning sun
What is death but four score
And barely ten?
Where is Goodness born
But in the hearts of men?
No Laws or King's command
Can stay a lover's hand
Or bid the winds to blow
Or a precious rose to grow
Death will come soon
Disguising his smile
Tarry a while
With music and song
Gossip and Hate are with us too long."

I looked at Robert's coffin and my mind sang to him, *you bloody beauty, you've escaped the dead hand of your mother!* Helen sat stiffly twisting a handkerchief in her hands. For the first time I noted her painted fingernails. She was staring fixedly ahead, tears streaming down her face and she made no attempt to brush them away. Then she turned and smiled bleakly.

"Gossip and Hate are with us too long."

There was total silence in that little church with its stations of the cross marching around the white wooden walls. The counter-tenor bowed while everyone quietly tried to hide their tears. Helen reached across and surreptitiously wiped a tear from my cheek. Dinny Dinham must have been the only man left dry eyed but he had served his time in the land of death and disablement.

"Gossip and Hate are with us too long."

The singer finished and silence descended like fog. He walked quickly to the coffin and slowly kissed it. A hum of surprise resonated quietly around the pews. Father Copeman's face drained a bloodless white as he stood awkwardly on one foot and then another before sprinkling holy water on the coffin with more than the usual energy, warding off the unpredictable world.

It was a day of sadness but a day of surprises. This was looking like the funeral to end all funerals. The biggest surprise of them all were the pall bearers. They were nothing like the usual professional po-faces that would have frightened the dead back to life. All six of them were handsome young men, most with dyed blonde hair and physiques that would have cost a fortune in gym memberships.

The priest obviously didn't go in for gym memberships. His stood back in shocked surprise for a moment as they came down the aisle. His thin hands fluttered like white cabbage moths as he tried to wave them away. By now, there was a rising whispering and humming from the congregation and people were craning their necks to see what was going to happen next. The pall-bearers ignored the priest. They paused with their backs to the congregation to allow more musicians to walk up to the coffin. One musician carried a tuba and two had violins. All were in dark suits and colourful bow ties. They began playing a type of Dixieland with unusual timing and a pause, the funeral march of old New Orleans.

By now Father Copeman was transfixed as if the Devil himself had leapt from the altar.

"Jesus. I've seen it all. The wars of religion." Dinny said under his breath. I wondered how Dinny fitted theology into his busy schedule.

In front of us the six pall bearers turned to pick up the coffin and that's when all hell broke loose in wonderful way. The pall bearers wore bow ties too but, apart from the struggling tuxedos, they were shirtless, exposing bronzed, oiled, muscled pecs at the front of their open suit coats.

They began a long slow funeral march to the beat of the tuba but paused at the appropriate beat to sway and step sideways with the coffin then sachet forward again, repeating the steps like a slow funeral dance...You could hear people talking and even giggling, then many burst into applause and started clapping in time.

I looked around and joined the motley crew that had packed out this little country church as we sent Robert Francis de Lacey Mandeville on his way in the special style that he owned like a fine leather glove.

That afternoon we held Robert's wake which meant we watched the coffin in the black hearse drive away for the private funeral. It looked like a lonely journey with Robert's body inside and grim face reapers his only companions. But, it was Robert's wish that the corporeal part of him be disposed as soon as possible, into the flames. We stood and watched the slow drive through the poplars and blackwoods lining the still green paddocks in the late afternoon sun. Cows grazed and birds went on with their bird lives and we drifted inside the local hall, which like the church was a white painted timbered building with the interior walls lined in old Baltic pine.

The only memory of Robert was his photograph on the tiny stage that must have seen a lot of school concerts and CWA flower shows over the years. No-one from *Coming Now* was there.

People drank and a country spread of lamingtons, cheese on biscuits, sausage rolls, cream cakes and tea gradually gave way to the barrel being opened and wine being placed on the long white tables. The homeless and the homeful drank together and people drifted around in that self-conscious twilight world that accompanies a departure.

My old band *Ship Creek* had agreed to provide the music and the young guy who, unannounced, had sung at the funeral was going to sing with us.

"He was a bloody beauty, mate." An old digger I'd seen around town was standing there with a cup of tea trembling dangerously in his hand. His bleary red eyes looked me up and down. "Do I know you?'

"I was Robert's boss."

He patted me on the arm. "Good on ya." He said and walked away, unsteady on his feet.

I had seen Helen talking in groups. She looked distracted and had a high colour in her cheeks and she was avoiding me.

The hall was full when we started playing then the young singer joined us on stage.

"I was Robert's lover." He said by way of introduction.

"I guessed that."

"Andrew."

"Paddy. Want to sing?"

"Yes."

"What?"

Paul, our lead guitarist, who never knew Robert, talked about songs and keys and we hummed Paul Kelly's and Kev Carmody's

From Little Things Big Things Grow. I wondered how we were going to get through it. It was easier for the others in the group because they didn't know Robert.

Andrew said, between verses. "Jesus. This is hard."

The story line of *From Little Things Big Things Grow* actually had a strange relevance with Robert de Lacey Malahide, British posh boy in permanent exile. Handing back white man's land to the original owners and the pouring of red earth by Prime Minister Gough Whitlam into the hands of Vincent Lingiarri was a good memorial for Robert and a lot of un-named people.

Sometimes on stage you never look at the audience and I avoided it until the old Digger came to the front of the stage to hear better. Behind him, were other battlers who had even less but, that day, they were standing alongside people who had enough. This was not *Coming Now*'s world of rewarded affluence and aspirational thinking.

Then we sang a piece that Andrew had written.

"When the poor come knocking on your door
Just let them in
When a hand is held
It means you've told the world
To let them in, to let them in"

We finished and I walked outside to find Helen. She was standing alone in copse of old oaks near boundary. She turned away from me as I approached.

"Helen. I know what you're thinking."

She turned, red faced and eyes filling with tears again. I reached out to touch her arms and she pulled back.

"Do you? Do you fucking know?" Both her hands were hanging by her side. Then, she wiped her nose with her hands.

"Yes. I do. No more hinting and self-protective bullshit, right? If you are not going to tell me. I'm going to say it and you can accept it or reject what I'm saying. Right?"

She tossed her head as if that was doomed to failure. I could see the still wet tearstains on her simple plain dress.

"You think I should have dropped *Coming Now* a long time ago, yes?" I said.

"Yes."

"You think they killed Robert?"

"Yes."

"And I plan to do nothing about it?"

"Absolutely. I think you're piss weak."

"Bit hard to prove."

"You're proving it now."

"No, I mean it's very hard to prove that *Coming Now* killed Robert. I can tell you Dinny will not let up on it. Never. Nor will I."

She looked at me and shook her head. "I've heard all that sort of stuff before. I've seen a few inquiries and I know what gets pushed under the carpets so don't tell me what will or will not happen."

I looked at my feet as music from the band drifted down the gravel drive and out into the soft summer air. There was still a smell of damp green pasture and even mist gathering near a dam on the farm next door. Some of the mourners were drifting out to their cars, easing themselves back into their own lives. The mini-bus that brought the homeless people was still empty though, except for the driver who sat with his feet on the dashboard reading *The Mercury*.

I leaned closer to Helen. She was caught between hesitation and rejection of me.

"We will pay back."

"Oh yeah?"

"We will pay back and we will pay them back not only for Robert but for what they are going to do for this country. OK?"

She nodded tentatively.

I said. "We will finish the *Coming Now* project."

"No. Never!"

"Hear me out. The pre-selection's this weekend. This is our last operation for *Coming Now.*"

"What about the election proper if Tommy Rayfinger gets pre-selected?"

"What about it?'

She looked at me very carefully as if I had a gun behind my back. "You're up to something aren't you?"

I glanced around and whispered in her ear. She was very still.

"Yes." She said quietly.

"And the drones? The *Coming Now* demonstration of their delivery drones. You're sure they've got permission to demonstrate with thirty drones in a public place?"

"I'm sure. I read the emails. It's all go." She said.

"Can you do it?"

Her smile was bleak. "That's what I did for a living. I got pretty good at it, you know."

TWENTY

Birds in the air carry the voice

Friday night at Dinny Dinham's was a fresh new experience for me. It was after tea time as Dinny called it and the replays of World Champion Wrestling were on.

"You've made a miracle," His wife Rhonda said as she ushered Helen and me into the house. "Ordinarily, he won't even take a phone call when the wrestling's on."

"Rhonda, it's on DVD. He can watch any time he likes."

She wiped her hands on her apron and snorted with laughter. "Yeah, well, you tell him that. He says it settles him down at the end of the week." She nodded at Helen who was cradling her laptop.

"In the bedroom love, there's a connection there."

"Stop talking about me." Dinny called from the great bout in the lounge room. Dinny and Rhonda's tidy weatherboard house in Glenorchy was their first and only home and will one day be converted into a 1980's museum. Patterned wall paper, frosted glass doors, a kitchen for eating in so that the big TV room could have space big enough for the electric powered Lazyboy reclining chairs to watch World Championship Wrestling and Crawford crime re-runs. Plenty of indoor plants in hanging baskets and cane chairs on the glassed in veranda gave you a good view of the two man ferns plonked symmetrically on the front lawn.

Dinny was in a tracksuit of bilious lime green so that it looked like a St. Patrick's Day float had invaded the Lazyboy in which he sat with his legs up.

"Hello, Dinny." Helen said from the kitchen.

"Go away. I don't even know you're here." Dinny said and didn't turn the volume down as Mario Milano threw Hulk Hogan to the canvas. We needed a place where Helen could program her plans for the next day, somewhere out of sight but with a secure connection.

We waited until Helen had left the room.

"Don't you love it?" Dinny said indicating the other Lazyboy. I sat down just as Hulk Hogan broke the hold and recovered enough to throw Mario Milano against the ring rope.

"Mate, that match was held forty years ago. They're both in an old people's home now." I said and ignored the bowl of crisps offered me.

"Yeah. And you watch opera. This acting is Academy Award compared with that bullshit."

"I heard that. Wash your mouth out," Rhonda called from the kitchen.

"Sorry love." He helped himself to the crisps. "Now, we're watching the wrestling right? I don't want to hear anything about your mate. Right?" He stared at me.

"Right."

"Goodo."

"But you're gonna drop the case?"

"I'm dropping nothing. Jeez! You bloody civvies, you watch too many bad movies. You like everything worked out nice and neat in the court where the villain gets his just deserts. Well. I'm telling you, it doesn't often work out like that, except in the bloody novels."

"Meaning?"

He turned the volume up and the wrestling crowd was already in hysterics as Hulk Hogan collared the referee and used him to batter the reeling Mario Milano. Somehow, Dinny was watching both the wrestling and me.

"Meaning. We may never know what happened and you'd better get used to that."

I leaned closer. "Dinny, are you giving up on Robert."

"Jesus mate! Lower your voice. No, I'm never gonna give up on this one. You've got my word. But, for now and maybe a long time, you're gonna have to sort it out yourselves."

"Sort it out?"

Dinny exhaled like a stranded whale and turned the volume up higher. "Yeah sort it out. Do I have to spell it out? What you gotta do is to hit them where it hurts. They want the money and they want the power. They're not gonna get an attack of the conscience and they'll have shit-hot lawyers if it ever gets to court. So hit the money and the power, that's their soft spot, down there." He pointed the remote control at his bunched up crotch.

"That's it?"

He shrugged. "That's it. But remember, whoever it was that organised it all. They never leave a trace and you don't know when they're coming. So you and your pretty mate, just do it right. I mean subtle."

"Dinny. Could you spell that word?"

"You want a cup of tea while your intellectual superior fiddles with that laptop?"

I shook my head and picked up a photo from the polished sideboard. It was the Hobart Football Club 1985 and a long haired Dinny was standing in the group photograph desperately trying to flex his puny muscles to compete ingloriously with the older working class blokes in the line-up.

"Nice mullet mate and those shorts. Wonder you could move in them." I said.

"That was the year before I joined the cop force. Never saw hair like that on me again."

We watched the TV melee in silence until we could hear Helen and Rhonda talking in the kitchen. Helen said *I shouldn't laugh* and starting laughing again, which was a break from the last few days.

"It's an insult to the human intelligence." Dinny said.

"What?"

He pointed at the wrestling. "They're gonna feature Abdullah the Butcher next week. The stretch plum, it's a fake move. Bloody fake!"

"I'll leave you to it." I said and propelled myself from the Lazyboy.

Helen was standing with her laptop under her arm and Rhonda was having a secret cigarette near the open kitchen window.

"OK?" I said.

They were both grinning.

"Yeah. I'm OK, Hamlet." Helen said.

I looked at Rhonda. "You are such a big mouth."

"Somebody's got to tell the truth around here." She said and they started to laugh again while Rhonda coughed and waved her hands to drive the smoke out the window.

In the car, Helen punched me lightly in the arm. "Hamlet. Oh my God!"

"Yeah. That was a long time ago." I said.

"A long time ago? It was only three years ago."

We could see the lights of the Zinc Works and the curving Tasman Bridge that was knocked down by an ore carrier in the unlucky days.

"It was before I met you."

"I would hope so." She laughed again. "No wonder you lost so much business. The whole bloody world must have known about you and your client's missus. And the dinner party in Sandy Bay, you and him, rolling on the table, wine spilling and the dishes crashing.

I love it! Why did he call you Hamlet Head before he reached over and dragged you onto the table? C'mon, I can keep a secret."

"I do not respond to gossip."

"Oh. That's not gossip. It sounds like real Hobart history to me. You know, I thought growing up with a drunken dad who embarrassed us every evening on his way back from the pub was bad but World Champion Wrestling in upper class Sandy Bay has to take the cake. Fucking the clients' wives. Great business model."

"Are you finished?"

She stroked my arm. "Yeah. I'm finished...Hamlet Head." She started laughing again.

"You happy with the programing?" I changed the subject but I could see the humour in it. Upsetting privileged people didn't seem such an issue now because they didn't pay the bills and tomorrow was a new day. But we still had a little job to do to make sure that a worse mob wasn't going to join that privileged club.

She stopped laughing and tapped the laptop. "As right as right can be. I've copied in the program to Dinny's computer just so I've got a back-up."

"Does Dinny know?"

"Well, he knows and he doesn't know. It's all set to delete and scoot on Sunday. No hard drive record." She said.

"I'll never cross you."

"You'd better believe it."

We were following the city streets which got busier the closer you got to the wharves and the fishing and cruise boats. It was a far cry from the neat homes like Dinny and Rhonda's where the homebodies had eaten their tea and settled down to TV and talk or quiet drinks with neighbours.

On the lawns of Parliament House people walked in the park beneath the autumn leaves of the oak trees. It was a true Friday night

with drinkers gathering across the road, outside the Customs House
and the Telegraph like feeding free range piglets. Women in tight
skirts and impossible high heels looked at blokes with pants so tight
they would make you sterile, barmen and waitresses dreaming of the
moment when they could sweep up and close the doors, loud boof-
heads shouting when a whisper would do, mating rituals, braying
like donkeys, lonely out-riders trying to look cool, spilt drinks and
violently coloured cocktails, all the ants at play before winter crept
in. Not one would have had an inkling of the next day's big surprise,
the famous Salamanca Incident, courtesy of Paddy Kennedy and
Associates; well, courtesy of former Sergeant Helen Troy, defender
of Australia and her drone kingdom.

"You know, I might be a little bit in love with you," Helen said
suddenly.

"What?"

"You heard me."

"Well, I might just feel the same way about you."

"Don't go overboard Hamlet Head."

"Well compared with some of your blokes, I'm probably looking
good."

"Don't kid yourself. Well, actually you are correctisimo. Wow,
have I fallen for some genuine AI doofuses! Nice to have someone
who is half way sane."

"Thanks."

"Maybe a teeny weeny bit up themselves."

"Don't get too romantic."

"I am. But we're not going to sleep together tonight. I'm very
much on edge."

"Understandable."

She laughed and pulled my ear. "Yeah. We're big on the romance.
Us two. Would you fight over me at a Sandy Bay dinner party, fall

all over the crayfish bisque and the organic mashed potato and the cheeky Pinots? Would you?"

"Yes. I would. I hate crayfish bisque."

"Good Samaritans." Helen said.

"What? Them?" I indicated the pub crowd.

She cradled the laptop on her knees. "No, people we know. Good Samaritans. That's why we're doing this thing tomorrow. For the Good Samaritans like Robert and Donna and your mate Dinny and Rhonda. That's who."

TWENTY-ONE

The dust returns to Earth

Big days in people's lives come and go. It's not always tents and circuses and trumpets. Sometimes the big decisions just creep up on people in non-descript places.

The town of Ross in Tasmania's Midlands fitted the bill. Nice town with convict buildings and a bridge that draws the tourists. Tasmanians come for the scallop pies. The bakery was doing good business. But Ross is not Disneyland.

The Town Hall still had the eternal gun carriage mounted as a war monument and tourists wandered round looking for something to take home. Ross and wool go together so do high prices for high quality sweaters and socks. Ladies in tartan skirts with large pins ran the place like a laird's estate and the local pub sported tartan carpets and a stags head staring mournfully at drinkers.

On the way up from Hobart we coached Tommy on the phone.

"Why are we going soft on gay marriage?" He asked.

"Tommy are you in the car on your own?"

"No. Tammy's here."

"Ok. You say that you believe a marriage is between a man and a woman. That's ok. But don't promise to bring a vote on it back to Parliament. That issue is dead. So, where do you stand on climate change?"

"I didn't like your talking points." Tommy said.

"He doesn't like your talking points." Tammy said.

"What about imprisoning refugees on Manus Island?"

There was a pause. "I'll follow the party policy on that. But, Australia should decide who comes here and the grounds on which they stay."

"Good. Now be very, very strong on family. Families are the lynchpin of Australian society."

"You betcha!" Tommy said.

"We've set up the video for you. You speak first then you run the video. You know how to work it?"

"Hooley dooley. I can work a video."

"OK. Just checking. Just press run and you're away. Like the newspapers this morning? There'll be a lot of journos there today. You are big news Tommy. They all want a copy of the video. I forgot to ask. That's OK?"

"That's ok." Tammy said.

"That's ok." Tommy said.

"Good luck." I touched off and we drove in silence for a time. On the seat were all the front page stories we'd fed to the media.

FOOTY GREAT SEEKS LIB PRESELECTION

RAYFINGER TO ENTER PARLIAMENT

RAYFINGER LIB FRONT RUNNER

Robert's photos were striking. Pastor Rayfinger was handsome enough at the best of times but two of the newspapers had taken what Robert used to call his Vaseline shot which was a Hollywood close-up with softened edges as if the front page should have carried his signature scrawled across the pic. *The Advocate* carried a shot of Tommy's greatest mark of the Grand Final which might have said something.

Towards the middle of the paper was a photo of Squeaky who

was holding a drone. The headline said *NEW DELIVERY FOR FAST FOOD JUST THE START SAYS TASSIE GROUP*. The rest of the story featured Tommy telling the world that new technologies would be delivering not only coffee, fast food, books and CDs, but jobs as well. We liked that part of our media release.

Helen waited a while then switched to commercial radio which we hoped would sex up the story and they delivered.

A Tasmanian technology company has promised two thousand new jobs within three years if it is able to gain official permission for its new delivery drones to make deliveries in urban areas. Coming Now President Tommy Rayfinger says that today's demonstration in Hobart's Salamanca Place will use twenty drones to deliver free hamburgers and coffee plus those two thousand new jobs. Mr Rayfinger said this was a major first since the new Coming Now system will hit the market without a single dollar of Government money. The announcer then added his own message. *Yes. Not a single dollar of tax-payers money. Now that's a new one. All we can say is good luck Tommy Rayfinger and the Coming Now team.*

Helen shook her head. "I wish you'd let me put our name to that media release. I know, I know. On this one, no way."

At the town hall in Ross it was low key. Tommy's black SUV was parked under the plane trees that ran the full gamut of the street. A handful of journalists were standing around. Most were pretty young but it was easy to tell them from the Liberal Party activists who walked self-consciously from their parked cars into the hall. Tommy and Tammy were out the front meeting and greeting with Tommy standing like a giraffe lowering its head to connect with other forest creatures. I saw George Rathbone ambling in, wearing a Harris tweed jacket over his checked shirt. I looked away because we were under strict instructions not to make it look like a travelling caravan manipulating candidate Pastor Tommy Rayfinger. Some young tyros in smart suits drifted amongst the journos, donating enough smiles to help their careers along. One was a Senator and another a senior party official. I could see a table up front with a neat white cloth on it. It was a strange atmosphere. Here was a whole career in public life being affected and the place looked like a meeting of the local farming improvement group.

"Do journalist ever get off their phones?" Helen said.

"They won't today. That's for sure."

"After all that preparation and hype and tactics and content and bullshit. Here we are in some..."

"Don't say it. A voter might hear you." We both had a wry laugh about that.

Helen tapped the newspapers. "Something big is gonna happen today and it's played out in a little corner of Tassie somewhere."

"Yep. Gavrilo Princip."

She peered at the journalists and pre-selectors. "Where?"

"He was the guy who shot Archduke Ferdinand and started the First World War."

"Well he's not here today. What was the point you're making?"

"Well he was walking back from a failed assassination attempt, pistol still in hand. He was in a side street when round the corner came the Archduke's car. The chauffeur had taken the wrong turn. Bang and nine million people died. Started in the back street of a back water."

"You're a bloody idiot." She smiled. She still had those fine lines around her mouth, donated by the sand and sun of the Middle East. "When can we go in?"

"We can't. But get close to the door. Quietly."

We waited until the meeting was well underway then sidled up to the door of the meeting. There was another candidate pushing his line about family life and the need to keep Australia for Australians.

It looked like family life was going to get a mawkish beating today. The questions started but I couldn't hear them because Dee Wadley spied me and pulled out her notebook. Helen moved closer to the door to listen better.

Dee opened her note book. "Oh hello stranger. I think you have a horse in this race, or so I'm told."

"No horse in this race." I said.

"Oh, why are you here?" she said suspiciously. "I heard you did have a horse."

"No horse." I said

"Got a tip then?"

"Yep. Be nice to your mother." Dee had once sold me out on a front page scoop I gave her.

"Well. We've been told that we can expect something very big."

I said. "What's that?"

She smiled deviously. We danced around each other until she admitted that a definite front page scoop was coming which even the print media could still make gold from after the evening television ran with the story.

There was polite applause from inside and someone closed the door. We could hear Tommy's base baritone announcing the wonder of family life, public decency, the power of belief in the Almighty and the Liberal party in that order, which got a good laugh. Then there was applause, not the type of hype Tommy was used to but strong enough to suggest that it would take someone very hot to beat him. I felt a strong nervousness in the pit of my stomach. I crossed my fingers and gestured hopefully at Helen who was almost ear against door. We could hear the theme music of Tommy's video as a deep voice told the world that families come first.

Then all hell broke loose.

If the Liberal panel for Lyons was ever going to reach the pinnacle of excitement, this was their day. We could hear the moaning first then the cries of joy and I knew it wasn't the panel members who were performing that age old ritual.

"Yes! Argh, Argh! Come on big boy! Give it to me! That's right, give it to me!"

"Look at the camera! Look at the camera!" Tommy's sexually heightened and urgent voice could penetrate walls which meant the journalists were well prepared when their smart phones began buzzing and pinging and the feed from the video inside went directly to their screens. For once, competition between them flew out the window. They clustered and showed each their screens as if they still couldn't believe what was before their eyes. Nor could the Chinese tourists who were still looking for scallop pies and warm woolen socks but found instead some strange Tasmanian customs.

Dee Wadley took her eyes off the screen long enough to point an accusatory finger at me but she didn't come over. She was too busy sending the whole video to her editors. The others were following suit. By the look of it, there wasn't a lot of interest in the rest of the voice over from Tommy's presentation. That was the bit we added about the exploitation of under-age employee volunteers by religious charities knocking off their commercial competitors. They were still sending their scoop when the door opened and Tommy plunged through the journalists' huddle. Their voices followed him all the way to his car. For a brief second, I saw Tammy Rayfinger turn, looking around until her eyes fixed for a moment on me. You can never be sure, but it was a *we're equal now* look. I nodded and she stepped delicately into the car as the Rayfingers drove away into the history books.

Helen turned and smiled a bleak smile. "For Robert." She said quietly.

"For Robert. Now one more to go."

We drove to the park near the old stone bridge and Helen took out her laptop and started punching in numbers and vectors. There was some interference but she played with it and the screens came to life. A swarm of drones was in the air, being captured on video by the drone in the rear. Their passage was slow due to the larger than usual payload of coffee and hamburgers that would in a few minutes be delivered to the Salamanca Markets as a demonstration of *Coming Now*'s capacity to revolutionise the delivery market. We watched them move in a bird like flock along the wide river, over Mount Rumney and the wooded Eastern Shore and then, in a slow wide sweep, cross back over the curving Tasman Bridge and baronial Government House with its incongruous cows grazing in the shade of the oak trees. The sky was clear and the Salamanca Markets would be full. A large cruise ship was already in the harbor and the mountain above the city was outlined as if in pencil. It was post card day for a post card event.

Helen said ok and the whole fleet turned towards the Salamanca Markets. You could make out the tents and crowds in the cafes of the old Georgian sandstone buildings. A vintage car rally with brightly coloured vehicles was parked on the lawns of Parliament House. The vision was so good that you could clearly make out the Citroens from the Jaguars and grosser Mercedes and black Fords displayed nose to nose.

"Got it!" She was biting her lips with the concentration.

"You're in control?" I said.

"You betcha. Got the lot." She moved the cursor with her long fingers and the entire fleet with the exception of the camera surveillance drone headed across the Market. The sound was low key but you could see people below looking up from the pathways between the canvas tents. There were about ten thousand visitors that day so there was a great audience for *Coming Now*'s demonstration of

Delivery Now, the Job Maker and the other business projects that *Coming Now* was going to spring on seventeen electorates around Australia. The press had already run some lengthy pieces yesterday on the Saturday demonstration so it was a big deal.

"They're trying to reprogram the system so we gotta go now. OK?" She said. Her face was grim and determined as she moved the cursor to wrest back control from the *Coming Now* crew back in Bagdad.

That's when culinary mayhem ruined *Coming Now* and Big Friend and anything else that giant organization had in mind for Australia; all happening on that Saturday in what was later to be known as the Salamanca Incident.

Suddenly the lead drone started to lower the coffee and hamburgers from about twenty metres above. Helen tapped an icon and the first load of hamburgers and coffee was dumped on the roadway. We had delayed the squadron long enough for the coffee to get cold.

"OK babies. Do your thing." Helen said and the squadron moved across the market, some tipping their contents from well above the market people. Other drones came in like a Pearl Harbour revival, tipping the messy tomato sauce laden contents on the fleeing citizens of Hobart. Tourists and musicians looked up and fled also, wondering what made Tasmania such a fascinating but dangerous place.

"The future is technology, Big Friend," Helen poked her head out the window and pumped her fists and laughed for the first time in weeks.

You could still see people running in all directions. A camera man appeared and was pointing upwards. Another joined him but, this time, trained his lens on the watching or running crowd. Like all major incidents there would be those who observed it all and there were a hell of a lot more who were trying to discipline kids or looking for parking meter change when it all happened.

"Don't Helen. That's a 1934 Citroen Traction Avant."

"Yes. Paddy. No more Ms. Nice Guy. No seriously, this is DGPS, it can be piloted to within a centimetre."

She moved the cursor again, her mouth wide open in concentration. She was obviously manoeuvring the camera drone to follow the other twenty as closely as possible. The TV cameras were now trained exclusively at the host of buzzing plastic and metal above them.

"Yep." She said and clicked. We watched as the twenty drones lifted and swooped in a swarm until they were circling and dipping above the forecourt of Parliament House, away from the cars on the lawn. The drones were taking different individual trajectories but they were in concert like a rising of the ephemeraoptera, the red spinners that rise in the Highland lakes and live only for a day or two. Finally, Helen had them in a circling flight path that showed the whole twenty in a perfect stacked formation like a major airport. She manipulated one to swoop over the forecourt and clear the spectators who soon got the message and moved back.

"OK." She clicked again and the entire *Coming Now* fleet that was going to change how Australia lives, tumbled and dived onto the Parliament forecourt, with front page impact.

"I'm gonna buy it." Lenny Lucic said.

Two weeks after the Rayfingers left town and the Liberal Party demanded that all future candidates sign a moral code to ensure that they truly represented hard working Australian families, Helen and I stood outside the locked gates of the *Coming Now* compound. The sign said FOR SALE and another said PLA SECURITY NO ENTRY. I looked around the silent deserted compound and the school with no kids and turned the phone onto speaker so that Helen could hear.

"Lenny. Why would you want to buy a church and a school and playing fields in the middle of no-where?"

"Mate, Mate. I'm gonna turn it into a tourist accommodation camp for all those religious groups and political parties and sports training groups. And there's subdivision potential with all the facilities there. It has even got a church and if they don't wanna pray there they can play there. We'll turn it into a casino. It's a bloody gift mate so I've made a formal offer and they've got seven days to accept or pull out. I want you bad mate to make this happen. I'll cut you into a big piece of the action cause you got a lot of friends in those Lefties."

Helen shook her head vigorously and whispered something in my ear.

"Lenny, just a second mate."

Helen shook her head again and said softly. "Not this place, please."

I shrugged. *A new town close to Hobart with a church and playing fields and sports facilities and cheaper housing and a place for the homeless. Light rail link. Close to the Brighton Industrial Hub. A New Jerusalem in Bagdad, a chance to do it right. Patrick Kennedy and Associates. New town developers. Doing it the right way in Malahide Town.*

Helen pointed a finger at me while Lenny explained how we would be cut into the deal and *didn't I have some influence in getting a casino licence and wasn't the light rail a great innovation and someone's gotta do something mate about affordable housing and wasn't it meant to be, you know a kind of miracle? Was I in or not?*

"Lenny. I'm interested but I will need to confer with my partner."

Helen gave a wave of disgust and walked along the fence line but she stopped and looked another sign. She spun around and ran back.

"Come and look. Just bloody come and look!" she said.

There it was. In that deserted compound with its ghosts and

empty school yards and silent church were five figures crouching and hiding and taking positions. Each was dressed in army fatigues but they were sadly topless like Vladimir Putin on one of his propaganda bear hunts.

"What the hell is that?"

Helen started laughing and clapping her hands like a child. "Read the sign."

The sign was a home-made job that promised *Paint Ball, healthy exercise, a chance to prove how tactical you are and an opportunity to pit yourself against those who stand in the way of your success*. The sign also had the price and a mobile number. The price of four sessions was two hundred dollars but that had been crossed out and the words, *discount value now fifty dollars* substituted in large red letters.

Over near the old aircraft hangers, the group had met head to head and emptied their magazines, flock, flock, berrup, crack and pop and were high-fiving each other like tribal fighters in some sad strange ritual.

"Huzzah! Huzzah!"

Then they broke into two groups and, ducking and weaving, took positions closer to us.

"Helen, ring the number."

Two forlorn figures, splattered in paint, stopped for a moment in the paint ball game. The tallest looked our way and almost snapped to attention. The other, was thinner and shorter but the face and the skinny torso were unmistakable. Lieutenant Squeaky (Army Reserve and discount paint ball entrepreneur) shouldered arms alongside his fellow officer in the Legion of the Lost, Brother Lester Underwood.

"You still there Paddy, my friend?" Lenny Lucic was becoming more desperate.

"I'm still here."

"Well mate, are you in or not?"

"Lennie. My partner and I are in as in can be." I said.

www.ingramcontent.com/pod-product-compliance
Lightning Source LLC
Chambersburg PA
CBHW032115020726
47494CB00007BA/2087